THE GRYB
A. E. van Vogt

NEW ENGLISH LIBRARY/TIMES MIRROR

First published in the USA in 1976 by Kensington Publishing Corp.

© 1976 by A. E. van Vogt and James H. Schmitz

First NEL Paperback Edition April 1980

NEL Books are published by
New English Library from
Barnard's Inn, Holborn,
London EC1N 2JR.
Made and printed in Great Britain by
William Collins Sons & Co Ltd
Glasgow

45004580 3

CONTENTS

THE GRYB

His eyes ached! He kept blinking them as he flew, striving to keep in sight the glitter of hurtling metal that was the power-driven spacesuit of his guide.

The man was desperately hard to see against the blazing brilliance of the remote disk of sun – incredibly small and gemlike sun, rising higher and higher from the fantastic horizon of Europa. It was almost, Thomas told himself, as if the guide was deliberately holding himself into the glare of the morning sun to distract his – Thomas's – wearying mind and dull his strength.

More than a mile below, a scatter of forest spread unevenly over a grim, forbidding land. Pock-marked rock, tortured gravel, and occasionally a sparse, reluctant growth of Jupiter grass that shone as brown and uninviting as the bare straggle of forest – and was gone into distance as they sped far above, two shining things of metal, darting along with the speed of shooting stars.

Several times Thomas saw herds of the tall, dapple-grey grass eaters below; and once, far to the left, he caught the sheeny glint of a scale-armoured, blood-sucker gryb.

It was hard to see his speedometer, built into the transparent headpiece of his flying space armour – hard because he had on a second headpiece underneath, attached to his electrically heated clothes; and the light from the sun split dazzlingly through the two barriers. But now that his suspicions were aroused, he strained his eyes against that glare until they watered and blurred. What he saw tightened his heavy jaw into a thin, hard line. He snapped into his communicators, his voice as cold and hard as his thoughts: 'Hey, you ahead there – what's your name? Barkett, Birkett – '

'Bartlett, sir!' a young man's voice sounded in his communicators; and it seemed to the older man's alert hearing that the accent on the 'sir' held the faintest suggestion of a

9

sneer, and a definite hostility. 'Ray Bartlett! What is it, sir?'

'You told me this trip would be five hundred and twenty-one miles or – '

'Or thereabouts!' The reply was swift, but the sneer was stronger, the hostility more apparent, more intentional.

Thomas's eyes narrowed to steely grey slits. 'You said five hundred and twenty-one miles. The figure is odd enough to be presumed exact, and there is no possibility that you would not know the exact distance from the Five Cities to the platinum mines. We have now travelled five hundred and twenty-nine miles – more every minute – since leaving the Five Cities a little over an hour ago, and – '

'So we have!' interrupted the young man with unmistakable insolence. 'Now isn't that too bad, Mr Famous Statesman Explorer Thomas.'

Thomas was silent, examining the situation for its potential menace. His first indignant impulse was to pursue the unexpected arrogance of the other, but his brain, suddenly crystal-clear, throttled the desire and leaped ahead in a blaze of speculation.

There was murder intent here. His mind ticked coldly, with a sense of something repeated; for the threat of death he had faced before, during those bold, tremendous years when he had roamed the farthest planets. It was icily comforting to know that this was but a repetition of what he had previously experienced – comforting to remember that he had conquered in the past. In murder, as in everything else, experience counted.

Thomas began to decelerate against the fury of built-up velocity. It would take time – but perhaps there still was time, though the other's attitude suggested the crisis was dangerously near. There was no more he could do till he had slowed considerably. Thomas quieted his leaping pulses and said gently:

'Tell me, is the whole community in on this murder? Or is it a scheme of your own?'

'There's no harm in telling you now!' Bartlett retorted. 'We knew in advance that your visit here was a farce. Ostensibly you came to find out for the Earth government if this moon of Jupiter was worth fighting about; actually, the government had decided in advance that they weren't going to fight, and you, with your terrific reputation, were to come here and put the thing over, pretending to be fair, but – '

His voice broke in a flare of hate: 'You sneaking coward! What about the folks who've been trying to make a living here, slaving, hoping, dreaming, planning, creating for the future? And for what! So that a bunch of cynical politicians can sell us down the river to a dirty, arrogant gang of Martians.'

Thomas laughed, a hard, humourless but understanding laugh that hid the slow caution with which he slanted towards the ground. The strain of the curving dive racked his body, tore at his lungs, but he held to it grimly.

He was alone in the sky now; the shining spacesuit of the guide had vanished into the dim distance. Evidently the man had not turned his head or noticed the deviation on his finder. Anxious for the discovery to be as long delayed as possible, Thomas said:

'So that's it. I see that I am now confronted with the emotional immaturities of a bunch of child minds. I wonder if the human race will ever grow up. Don't you know that at one time the world was divided into warring nations, and before that into fiercely patriotic States; and before that human beings owed their loyalties to towns? Will we always have such fools to contend with? Well-meaning fools, who understand nothing of political, social or vital economy, and are perpetually victims of their own undisciplined desires and emotional incoherencies.'

'Yah!' Ray Bartlett snarled. 'That kind of talk may go over big in the drawing-rooms of London and New York, but it's plain rot to the men and women who stand to lose their homes. You're going to die because we're not letting you get back with any lying story about Europa. We're going to fake up some notes in your handwriting – we've got a handwriting expert – and then we'll give the notes to the newspapers; and let the government try to back out after that. With you dead – '

Thomas asked grimly: 'And how are you going to kill me?'

'In about ten seconds,' the young man began tautly, 'your engine – ' He broke off. 'Hah, you're not behind me any more. So you're trying to land. Well, it won't do you any good, damn your soul! I'll be right back that way – '

Thomas was only fifty feet from the bleak rock when

11

there was a sudden grinding in the hitherto silent mechanism of his atomic motor. The deadly swiftness of what happened then left no time for more than instinctive action. He felt a pain against his legs, a sharp, tearing pain, a dizzy, burning sensation that staggered his reason – and then he had struck the ground – and with a wild, automatic motion jerked off the power that was being so horribly short-circuited, that was burning him alive. Darkness closed over his brain like an engulfing blanket –

The blurred world of rock swaying and swirling about him – that was Thomas's awakening! He forced himself to consciousness and realized after a moment of mental blankness that he was no longer in his spacesuit. And, when he opened his eyes he could see without a sense of dazzle, now that he had only the one helmet – the one attached to his electrically heated clothes. He grew aware of something – an edge of rock – pressing painfully into his back. Dizzily, but with sane eyes, he looked up at a lean-faced young man, who was kneeling beside him.

The young man – Ray Bartlett – returned his gaze with unsmiling hostility, and said curtly:

'You're lucky to be alive. Obviously you shut off the motor just in time. It was being shorted by lead grit, and burned your legs a little. I've put some salve on, so you won't feel any pain; and you'll be able to walk.'

He stopped and climbed to his feet. Thomas shook his head to clear away the black spots, and then gazed up at the other questioningly, but he said nothing. The young man seemed to realize what was in his mind.

'I didn't think I'd be squeamish with so much at stake,' he confessed almost roughly, 'but I am. I came back to kill you, but I wouldn't even kill a dog without giving him a chance. Well, you've got your chance, if it's worth anything.'

Thomas sat up, his eyes narrowed on the young man's face inside the other's helmet. Ray Bartlett was a handsome young fellow with a pleasing countenance that ordinarily must have been frank and open. It was an honest face, twisted now with resentment and a sort of dogged determination.

Frowning with thought, Thomas looked around; and his eyes, trained for detail, saw a lack in the picture.

'Where's your spacesuit?'

Ray Bartlett nodded his head skyward. His voice held no quality of friendliness as he said: 'If your eyes are good, you'll see a dark spot, almost invisible now, to the right of the sun. I chained your suit to mine, then gave mine power. They'll be falling into Jupiter about three hundred hours from now.'

Thomas pondered that matter-of-factly. 'You'll pardon me if I don't quite believe that you've decided to stay and die with me. I know that men will die for what they believe to be right. But I can't quite follow the logic of why you should die. No doubt you have made arrangements to be rescued.'

Ray Bartlett flushed, his face growing dark with the turgid wave of angry colour. 'There'll be no rescue,' he growled from his throat. 'I didn't like what you said about un-disciplined desires and emotional immaturities. I know what you meant – that we of the Five Cities were thinking selfishly of ourselves, blind to the general welfare. I'm going to prove to you that, in this matter, no individual in our community thinks of himself. I'm going to die here with you because, naturally, we'll never reach the Five Cities on foot, and as for the platinum mines, they're even farther away.'

'Pure bravado!' Thomas said. 'In the first place your staying with me proves nothing but that you're a fool; in the second, I am incapable of admiring such an action. However, I'm glad you're here with me, and I appreciate the salve on these burns.'

Thomas climbed gingerly to his feet, testing his legs, first the right, then the left, and felt a little sickening surge of dizziness that he fought back with an effort. 'Hm-m-m,' he commented aloud in the same matter-of-fact manner as before. 'No pain, but weak. That salve ought to have healed the burns by dark.'

'You take it very calmly,' said Ray Bartlett acridly.

Thomas nodded his powerfully built head. 'I'm always glad to realize I'm alive; and I feel that I can convince you that the course being pursued by the government of which I am a minister is the only sane one.'

The young man laughed harshly. 'Fat chance. Besides, it doesn't matter. You don't seem to realize our predicament. We're at least twelve days from civilization – that's figuring

13

sixty miles a day, which is hardly possible. Tonight, the temperature will fall to a hundred below freezing, at least, though it varies down to as low as a hundred and seventy-five below, depending on the shifting of Europa's core, which is very hot, you know, and very close to the surface at times. That's why human beings – and other life – can exist on this moon at all. The core is jockeyed around by the Sun and Jupiter, with the Sun dominating, so that it's always fairly warm in the daytime and why, also, when the pull is on the other side of the planet, it's so devilish cold at night. I'm explaining this to you, so you'll have an idea of what it's all about.'

'Go on,' Thomas replied without comment.

'Well, if the cold doesn't kill us, we're bound to run into at least one bloodsucker gryb every few days. They can smell human blood at an astounding distance; and blood for some chemical reason drives them mad with desire. Once they corner a human being it's all up. They tear down the largest trees, or dig into caves through solid rock. The only protection is an atomic gun, and ours went up with our suits. We've only got my hunting knife. Besides all that, our only possible food is the giant grass eater, which runs like a deer at the first sight of anything living, and which, besides, could kill a dozen unarmed men if it was cornered. You'll be surprised how hungry it is possible to get within a short time. Something in the air – and, of course, we're breathing filtered Europan air – speeds up normal digestion. We'll be starving to death in a couple of hours.'

'It seems to give you a sort of mournful satisfaction.' Thomas said dryly.

The young man flashed: 'I'm here to see that you don't get back alive to the settlement, that's all.'

Thomas scarcely heard him. His face was screwed into a black frown. 'The more you tell me, the more I am convinced that the human beings on Europa are a sorry lot, not true pioneers. They've been here fifty years, and they've built their cities with machines, and machine-operated their mines – and not a single individual has rooted himself in the soil. No one has learned to exist without the luxuries that were brought from Earth. You talk of their having slaved and created. Bah! I tell you, Ray Bartlett, this is a terrible indictment of these so-called pioneers of yours, who simply

14

moved the equivalent of an Earth city here and live an artificial life, longing for the day, no doubt, when they're wealthy enough to get back to the real thing.'

The young man retorted grimly: 'Yes. Well, you try living off the soil of this barren moon – try killing a gryb with your bare hands.'

'Not my hands,' replied Thomas as grimly. 'My brains and my experience. We're going to get back to the Five Cities in spite of these natural obstacles, in spite of you!'

In the silence that followed, Thomas examined their surroundings. He felt his first real chill of doubt as his eyes and mind took in that wild and desolate hell of rock that stretched to every horizon. No, not every! Barely visible in the remote distance of the direction they would have to go was a dark mist of black cliff.

It seemed to swim there against the haze of semi-blackness that was the sky beyond the horizon. In the near distance the piling rock showed fantastic shapes, as if frozen in a state of writhing anguish. And there was no beauty in it, no sweep of grandeur, simply endless, desperate miles of black, tortured *deadness* – and silence!

He grew aware of the silence with a start that pierced his body like a physical shock. The silence seemed suddenly alive. It pressed unrelentingly down upon that flat stretch of rock where they stood. A malevolent silence that kept on and on, without echoes, without even a wind now to whistle and moan over the billion caves and gouged trenches that honeycombed the bleak, dark, treacherous land around them. A silence that seemed the very spirit of this harsh and deadly little world, here under that tiny, cold, brilliant sun, little more than a dazzling, distorted point in the blue-black sky.

'Gets you, doesn't it?' Ray Bartlett said, and there was a sneer in his voice.

Thomas stared at him, without exactly seeing him. His gaze was far away.

'Yes,' he said thoughtfully. 'I'd forgotten what it felt like; and I hadn't realized how much I'd forgotten. Well, we'd better get started.'

As they leaped cautiously over the rock, assisted by the smaller gravitation of Europa, the young man said: 'Perhaps

15

you'll understand better how we, who've built cities and homes on this far-away moon, feel about the prospect of being handed over to another government?'

'I am not,' said Thomas curtly, 'prepared to discuss the matter with a person who does not understand psychology, sociology, history and political economy. There is nothing more futile than arguing with someone who has no basis for his opinions but a vague backwash of emotions.'

'We know what's right and what's human,' Ray Bartlett replied icily. 'We've got our scientists, too, and our engineers and teachers; and I'm here to see that their decision to kill you is carried out.'

'You have only a knife now,' Thomas commented, 'and if you attacked me with that I'd have to show you the method employed by the Martian plainsmen to disarm a man with a knife. It's very simple, really, and consistently effective.'

'Yeah!' Ray Bartlett said roughly, his lean face tight, his formidable body tense. 'What good would that do? I could still tear you apart with my bare hands.'

Thomas slowed in his swift walking to glance at the other. 'I venture to suggest that, with my wide experience in my favour, you could do nothing against me. However,' he said hastily as the young man's dark eyes flashed with unfriendly intent, 'I apologize for making a provocative remark. My words might properly be construed as a dare – in fact, all threats, however veiled behind apparent reason and moral uplift, are dares – and history teaches that such provocation produces an inevitable physical conflict. Tell me, what do you do for a living?'

'I'm a metal engineer!' Ray Bartlett said gruffly.

'Oh,' Thomas's voice held a note of pleased surprise. 'I see that I've been underestimating you. No one will understand better than you the metal end of this business of Mars taking over Europa.'

'Mars isn't taking over Europa!' Bartlett snapped. 'And don't try to pull any flattery about how easy it should be for me to undertsand your subtle reasoning. I can see through that kind of stuff.'

Thomas ignored him. 'Here are the figures. The earth uses ten billion tons of steel every year; Mars two billion – '

'That's proof,' Bartlett interjected, 'that they wouldn't

16

dare go to war with us, because even as it is, we sell them half their steel. If we cut that out, they couldn't maintain their industries to supply peacetime needs, let alone wartime. We can tell them to go stick it.'

'You're quite wrong. Your reasoning is that of a news-paper correspondent who totals up the armaments of opposing sides and then says, "Look, we've got more!" War is the great unknown, the unpredictable. A military genius with a million men can lick a proportionately well-armed two million men. Up to a certain point, war is a science like astronomy, then it becomes astrology. So far as science can help us, our general staff has decided that, strategically, we are in a bad way. While we do not actually believe we would lose, we could not guarantee a victory.'

'That is the argument of conservative old women. They wouldn't dare to fight.'

'Here's the breakdown of figures,' Thomas went on calmly. 'Half our steel, as well as the billion tons we sell to Mars, is mined with great difficulty on Jupiter. We couldn't operate those mines in case of war because the mines are hopelessly vulnerable to attack. That leaves us five billion. We couldn't operate the mines on Titan, which provide a scant fifty million tons of steel, and, of course, Europa would be captured within a month of the war's beginning. The reason for all this is that it is militarily impossible for our ships to maintain the spacelanes between Earth and Jupiter, except at certain seasons of the year, when Mars was on the other side of the Sun from Jupiter. The Martians, however, would not start the war until the situation was favourable to them.

'Now, naturally, the Martians won't be able to operate the Jupiter mines under war conditions, but they should have no difficulty continuing operations on Ganymede, Io, Callisto, as well as Europa after they take it, and Titan, after they take that. Meantime, we'd have the supplies of Venus, the Moon and Earth, sufficient to supply us with some four billion tons a year. Considering the greater size of Earth, and the larger populations on Venus and Earth, they, with their smaller normally necessary needs, would actually have the advantage of us with their twelve hundred million tons.

'And all these mighty forces would be unleashed into a trillion-dollar war for what? To retain a paltry hundred

17

million tons of steel – and other metals in proportion – from Europa. Naturally, we decided it wasn't worth it when we saw the way the political situation on Mars was tending towards one disastrous and inevitable end.'

'You damned cowards!' Ray Bartlett snarled. 'We're not fighting for steel. We're fighting to the last man and woman for our cities and our homes. Now, let's not talk about it any more. You make me sick with your cold, inhuman reasoning. Using human beings like pawns. Well, let me tell you, they're the only ones who count. Thank Heaven, you and I haven't a chance of getting out of this alive.'

Two hours later the Sun was high in those dark, gloomy heavens. It had been two hours of silence. Two hours while they tramped precariously along thin stretches of rock between fantastic valleys that yawned on either side, while they skirted the edges of caves whose bleak depths sheered straight down into the restless bowels of the moon. Two hours of desolation.

The great black cliff, no longer misted by distance, loomed near and gigantic. As far as the eye could see it stretched to either side; and from where Thomas toiled and leaped ever more wearily, its wall seemed to rear up abrupt and glassy and unscalable. He gasped:

'I didn't realize I was so out of condition. I hate to confess it, but I'm not sure I can climb that cliff.'

The young man turned a face towards him that had lost its brown healthiness in a grey, dull fatigue. A hint of fire came back into his dark eyes.

'It's hunger!' he said curtly. 'I told you what it would be like. We're starving.'

Thomas pressed on, but after a moment slackened his pace, and said: 'This grass eater – it also eats the smaller branches of trees, doesn't it?'

'Yes. That's what its long neck is for. What about it?'

'Is that all it eats?'

'That and Jupiter grass!'

'Nothing else?' Thomas's voice was sharp with question, his powerfully built face drawn tight with insistence. 'Think, man!'

Ray Bartlett bridled. 'Don't take that tone to me. What's the use of all this, anyway?'

'Sorry – about the tone, I mean. What does it drink?'

'It licks ice. They always stay near the rivers. During the brief melting periods each year, all the water from the forests runs into the rivers and freezes. The only other thing it eats or drinks is salt. Like Earth animals, they absolutely have to have salt, and it's pretty rare.'

'Salt! That's it!' Thomas's voice was triumphant. 'We'll have to turn back. We passed a stretch of rock salt about a mile back. We'll have to get some.'

'Go back! Are you crazy?'

Thomas stared at him, his eyes grey pools of steely glitter. 'Listen Bartlett, I said a while ago that I didn't think I could climb those cliffs. Well, don't worry, I'll climb them. And I'll last through all today, and all tomorrow and the other twelve or fifteen or twenty days. I've put on about twenty-five pounds during the last ten years that I've been a cabinet minister. Well, dammit, my body'll use that as food, and by Heaven, I'll be alive and moving and going strong when you're staggering like a drunken sailor. I'll be alive when you're dead and buried for a hundred miles. But if we expect to kill a grass eater and live decently, we've got to have salt. I saw some salt, and we can't take a chance on passing it up. So back we go.'

They glared at each other with the wild, tempestuous anger of two men whose nerves are on ultimate edge. Then Bartlett drew a deep breath and said:

'I don't know what your plan is, but it sounds crazy to me. Have you ever seen a grass eater? Well, it looks something like a giraffe, only it's bigger, and faster on its feet. Maybe you've got some idea of tempting it with salt, and then killing it with a knife. I tell you, you can't get near it – But I'll go back with you. It doesn't matter, because we're going to die, no matter what you think. What I'm hoping is that a gryb sees us. It'll be quick that way.'

'There is something,' said Thomas, 'pitiful and horrible about a young man who is determined to die.'

'You don't think I want to die!' the young man flashed. 'Why, I had everything to live for, until you came along with your miserable – '

His passionate voice died abruptly, but Thomas knew better than to let so much fierce feeling die unexplored.

'No doubt,' he ventured softly, 'there is a girl you love – '

19

He saw by the wretched look on the young man's face that he had struck home.

'Ah, well' said Thomas, 'she'll probably marry someone else. There's always a second man who desires to taste of the manifold delights and charms of a beautiful and intelligent girl.'

The young man said nothing; and Thomas realized his words had started a cruel train of thought in the other. He felt no compunction. It was absolutely imperative that Ray Bartlett develop a desire to live. In the crisis that seemed all too near now, his assistance might easily be the difference between life and death.

It was odd, the fever of talk that came upon Thomas as they laboriously retraced their steps to the salt rock. It was as if his tongue, of all his body, had become intoxicated; and yet his words, though swift, were not incoherent, but reasoned and calculated to convince the younger man:

'Look at it this way. Your people, over a period of fifty years, have built five cities, with a total population of a million. You produce from your mines a hundred million tons of steel, a thousand tons of platinum, and about a hundred million tons of other metals – about two hundred million tons altogether. Of course, that's per year.

'Now, your engineers pointed out that estimates of Europa's recoverable metals indicated that in a thousand years the supply will be exhausted. In other words, there are two hundred billion tons of metal on this little moon, equal to twenty years of the normal needs of Earth. The value of the entire thousand years' supply, at an average of twenty dollars per ton, is four thousand billion dollars. I need hardly tell you that a war between Earth and Mars would cost ten times that much for each year that it lasted, not counting the hundred to two hundred million lives that would be destroyed in every conceivable horrible manner, the brutalizing of minds that would take place, the destruction of liberty that would ensue. Did the leaders of your community consider that in their deliberations?'

'I tell you,' Ray Bartlett contended stubbornly, 'the Martians won't fight, if you stand up to them and – '

'You keep repeating that like a parrot!' Thomas snapped.

'The internal political situation on Mars has reached an explosive point. There are two groups on the planet – one ferociously hostile to Earth, the other – the government – believing in negotiation. We want that government to stay in power, but they haven't a chance in the elections this year unless they can show material progress. Europa will be their answer –'

'Here's your salt!' Bartlett interrupted him curtly.

The salt rock composed a narrow ledge that protruded like a long fence which ran along in a startlingly straight line and ended abruptly at a canyon's edge, the fence rearing up, as if cringing back in frank dismay at finding itself teetering on the brink of an abyss.

Thomas picked up two pieces of salt rubble and slipped them into the capacious pockets of his plainsmanlike coat – and started back towards the dark wall of cliff nearly three miles away. He took up the thread of his argument where he had left off:

'And remember this. It's not only Europa's recoverable metals that will be used up in a thousand years, but also the metal resources of the entire Solar System. That's why we must have an equitable distribution now, because we can't afford to spend the last hundred of those thousand years fighting over metal with Mars. You see, in that thousand years we must reach the stars. We must develop speeds immeasurably greater than that of light – and in that last, urgent, hundred years we must have their co-operation, not their enmity. Therefore they must not be dependent on us for anything; and we must not be under the continual mind-destroying temptation of being able to save ourselves for a few years longer if we sacrifice them.'

Ray Bartlett said, rage nearly choking his voice: 'I can see what you're trying to do – pretending that you're capable of thinking of the long-run welfare of the world. Well, forget it; you're not God. People get to believe they are, you know; and that they can so manipulate the strings of their puppet ideas and puppet men that everything will inevitably happen as they desire. But we're not puppets, we human beings. In a thousand years, anything can happen.'

He finished roughly: 'And now I tell you again to shut up! I don't want to hear your arguments. You said before that the basis of our beliefs is different. You're damned right it is. So shut up, damn you! I'm so hungry that I can hardly stand up.'

'Well,' Thomas asked wearily, 'what is the basis of your opinions? I am willing to debate on your basis.'

The young man made no answer. They trudged along in silence.

Thomas's body ached in every muscle and every nerve pulsed alarms to his brain. He clung with a desperate, stubborn strength to each bit of rock projecting from the cliff wall, horribly aware that a slip meant death. Once he looked down, and his brain reeled in black dismay from the fearful depths that fell away behind him.

Through blurred vision he saw the young man a few feet away, the tortured lines of his face a grim reminder of the hunger weakness that was corroding the very roots of their two precariously held lives.

'Hang on!' Thomas gasped. 'It's only a few more yards.'

They made it, and collapsed on the very edge of that terrific chasm of cliff, too weary to climb the gentle slope that remained before they could look over the country beyond, too exhausted to do anything but lie there, sucking the life-giving air into their lungs. At last Ray Bartlett gasped:

'What's the use? If we had any sense we'd jump off this cliff and get it over with.'

'We can jump into a deep cave any time,' Thomas retorted. 'Let's get going.'

He rose shakily to his feet, took a few steps, then stiffened and flung himself down with a hissing intake of his breath. His fingers grabbed the other's leg and jerked him back brutally to a prone position:

'Down for your life. There's a herd of grass eaters half a mile away. And they *mean* life for us.'

Bartlett crawled up beside him, almost eagerly; and the two peered cautiously over the knob of rock out into a grassy plain. The plain was somewhat below them, Thomas saw. To the left, a scant hundred yards away, like a wedge driven into the grassland, was the pointed edge of a forest. The grass beyond seemed almost like a projection of the forest growth. It, too, formed a wedge that petered out in bleak

22

rock. At the far end of the grass was a herd of about half a hundred grass eaters.

'They're working this way!' Thomas said. 'And they'll pass close to that wedge of trees.'

A faint fire of irony edged Bartlett's voice as he said: 'And what will you do – run out and put salt on their tails? I tell you, Thomas, we haven't got a thing that – '

'Our first course,' said Thomas, unheeding, seeming to think out loud, 'is to get into that thick belt of trees. We can do that by skirting along this cliff's edge, and putting the trees between us and the animals. Then you can loan me your knife.'

'OK!' the young man agreed in a tired voice. 'If you won't listen, you'll have to learn from experience. I tell you, you won't get within a quarter of a mile of those things.'

'I don't want to,' Thomas replied. 'You see, Bartlett, if you had more confidence in *life*, you'd realize that this problem of killing animals by cunning has been solved before. It's absolutely amazing how similarly it has been solved on different worlds, and under widely differing conditions. One would almost suspect a common evolution, but actually it is only a parallel situation producing a parallel solution. Just watch me.'

'I'm willing,' said Ray Bartlett. 'There's almost any way I'd rather die than by starving. A meal of cooked grass eater is tough going, but it'll be pure heaven. Don't forget, though, that the bloodsucker grybs follow grass-eater herds, get as near as possible at night, then kill them in the morning when they're frozen. Right now, with darkness near, a gryb must be out there somewhere, hiding, sneaking nearer. Pretty soon he'll smell us, and then he'll – '

'We'll come to the gryb when he comes for us!' said Thomas calmly. 'I'm sorry I never visited this moon in my younger days; these problems would all have been settled long ago. In the meantime, the forest is our goal.'

Thomas's outward calmness was but a mask for his inner excitement. His body literally shook with hunger and desire as they reached the safety of the forest. His fingers were trembling violently as he took Bartlett's knife and began to dig at the base of a great, bare, brown tree.

'It's the root, isn't it,' he asked unsteadily, 'that's so tough and springy that it's almost like fine tempered steel, and won't break even if it's bent into a circle? They call it eurood on Earth, and it's used in industry.'

'Uh-huh!' Bartlett agreed. 'What are you going to do – make a bow? I suppose you could use a couple of grass blades in place of catgut. The grass is pretty strong and makes good rope.'

'No,' said Thomas. 'I'm not making a bow and arrow. Mind you, I can shoot a pretty mean arrow. But I'm remembering what you said about not being able to get within a quarter of a mile of the beasts.'

He jerked out a root, which was about an inch in thickness, cut off a generous two-foot length, and began to sharpen, first one end, then the other.

It was hard going, harder than he had expected, because the knife skidded along the surface as if it was so much metal. Finally it obtained a cutting hold. 'Makes a good edge and point,' he commented. 'And now, give me a hand in bending this double, while I tie some grass blades around to keep it that way.'

'O-oh!' said Bartlett wonderingly. 'I see-e-e! Say, that is clever. It'll make a mouthful about six inches in diameter. The grass eater that gets it will gobble it up in one gulp to prevent any of the others getting the salt you're going to smear on it. His digestive juices will dissolve the grass string, the points will spring apart and tear the wall of his stomach, producing an internal haemorrhage.'

'It's a method,' said Thomas, 'used by the primitives of Venus to kill the elusive Paamer deer; the Martian plainsman kills the water gopher with it, and, last but not least, our own Eskimo back on Earth uses it on wolves. Naturally, they all use different kinds of bait, but the principle is the same.'

He made his way cautiously to the edge of the forest. From the shelter of a tree he flung the little piece of bent wood with all his strength. It landed in the grass a hundred and fifty feet away.

'We'd better make some more!' Thomas said. 'We can't depend on one being found.'

The eating was good; the cooked meat tough but tasty; and it was good, too, to feel the flow of strength into his body.

Thomas sighed at last and stood up, glanced at the sinking Sun, an orange-sized ball of flame in the western sky.

'We'll have to carry sixty Earth pounds of meat apiece; that's four pounds a day for the next fifteen days. Eating meat alone is dangerous; we may go insane, though it really requires about a month for that. We've got to carry the meat because we can't waste any more time killing grass eaters.'

Thomas began to cut into the meaty part of the animal, which lay stretched out on the tough grass; and in a few minutes had tied together two light bundles. By braiding grass together, he made himself a pack sack and lifted the long shank of meat until it was strapped to his back. There was a little adjustment necessary to keep the weight from pressing his electrically heated clothes too tightly against him; when he looked up finally, he saw that the young man was looking at him peculiarly.

'You realize, of course,' Bartlett said, 'that you're quite insane now. It's true that, with these heated suits, we may be able to live through the cold of tonight, provided we find a deep cave. But don't think for a second that, once a gryb gets on our trail, we'll be able to throw it a piece of sharpened wood and expect it to have an internal haemorrhage.'

'Why not?' Thomas asked; and his voice was sharp.

'Because it's the toughest creature ever spawned by a crazy evolution, the main reason I imagine why no intelligent form of life evolved on Europa. Its claws are literally diamond hard; its teeth can twist metals out of shape; its stomach wall can scarcely be cut with a knife, let alone a crudely pointed wood.'

His voice took on a harsh note of exasperation: 'I'm glad we've had this meal; starving wasn't my idea of a pleasant death. I want the quick death that the gryb will give us. But for Heaven's sake, get it out of your head that we shall live through this. I tell you, the monster will follow us into any cave, cleverly enlarge it wherever he has difficulty; and he'll get us because eventually we'll reach a dead end. They're not normal caves, you know, but meteor holes, the result of a cosmic cataclysm millions of years ago, and they're all twisted out of shape by the movement of the planet's crust. As for tonight, we'd better get busy and find a deep cave with plenty of twists in it, and perhaps a place where we can block the air currents from coming in. The winds will be arriving about a half-hour before the sun goes down, and our electric heaters won't be worth anything against those freezing blasts. It might pay us to gather some of the dead wood lying around, so we can build a fire at the really cold part of the night.'

Getting the wood into the cave was simple enough. They gathered great armfuls of it, and tossed it down to where it formed a cluttering pile at the first twist in the tunnel. Then, having gathered all the loose wood in the vicinity, they lowered themselves down to the first level, Thomas first in a gingerly fashion; the young man – Thomas noticed – with a snap and spring. A smile crinkled the lips of the older man. The spirit of youth, he reflected, would not be suppressed.

They were just finishing throwing the wood down to the next level when suddenly a shadow darkened the cave mouth. Thomas glanced up with a terrible start and had a fleeting glimpse of great fanged jaws and glowing eyes that glared from a hideous head; a thick red tongue licked out in unholy desire, and a spray of saliva rained down upon their transparent metal helmets and leather-like clothes. And then Ray Bartlett's leather-covered hands bit like sharp stones into Thomas's arm; he felt himself dragged over the edge.

They landed unhurt among the loose pile of branches below; and scrambled frantically to throw it farther down. A great mad clawing and horrible bass mewing above them whipped them to desperate speed. They made it, as that enormous head peered down from the second level, visible only by the phosphorescent glow of its eyes, like two burning coals a foot and a half apart.

There was a terrific scrambling sound behind the two men as they pushed wildly down to the next level; a rock bounced down, narrowly missing them as it clattered past; and then, abruptly, silence and continuing darkness.

'What happened?' Thomas asked in bewilderment.

There was bitterness in Ray Bartlett's voice as he replied: 'It's wedged itself in, because it's realized it can't get us in the few minutes left before it freezes for the night; and, of course, now we won't be able to get out past it, with that great body squeezed against the rock sides.

'It's really a very clever animal in its way. It never chases grass eaters, but just follows them. It has discovered that it wakes up a few minutes before they do; naturally, it thinks we, too, will freeze, and that it will wake up before we will. In any event, it knows we can't get out. And we can't. We're finished.'

All that long night, Thomas waited and watched. There were times when he dozed, and there were times when he thought he was dozing, only to realize with a dreadful start that the horrible darkness had played devil's tricks on his mind.

The darkness during the early part of the night was like a weight that held them down. Not the faintest glimmer of natural light penetrated that Stygian night. And when, at last, they made a fire from their pile of brush, the pale, flickering flames pushed but feebly against the pressing, relentless force of the darkness and seemed helpless against the cold.

Thomas began to notice the cold, first as an uncomfortable chill that ate into his flesh, and then as a steady, almost painful, clamminess that struck into his very bones. The cold was noticeable, too, in the way white hoar-frost thickened on the walls. Great cracks appeared in the rock; and not once, but several times, sections of the ceiling collapsed with a roar that threatened their lives. The first clatter of falling debris seemed to waken Bartlett from a state of semi-coma. He jerked to his feet; and Thomas watched him silently as he paced restlessly to and fro, clapping his gloved, heated hands together to keep them warm.

'Why not,' Thomas asked, 'go up and build a fire against the gryb's body? If we burn him – '

'He'd just wake up,' Bartlett said tersely, 'and besides, his hide won't burn at ordinary temperatures. It has all the properties of metallic asbestos, conducts heat, but is practically noncombustible.'

Thomas was silent, frowning; then: 'The toughness of this creature is no joke – and the worst of it all is that our danger, the whole affair, has been utterly useless. Fake handwriting or not, my colleagues will know the truth and will suspect foul play. Rumours to that effect will spread automatically through the press and develop into open vilification of the murderous Five Cities. Before you know it, there will be a swelling murmur of demand for retribution; and in such a

27

dark atmosphere it will be the simplest matter in the world to hand Europa over to Mars. You think that's far-fetched, don't you?'

'It's crazy!' half whispered Ray Bartlett shakily.

'You may not realize it even now,' Thomas went on, 'but the person to have concentrated upon was myself. I don't think I am exaggerating when I say that any solution which I proposed would have been accepted. My reputation has been the conduct of a peculiar set of circumstances, but, once established, it acquired rocklike qualities. The report of my death will create a sensation and have all the effects that I have described.'

'Well, what should we have done?' Ray Bartlett exclaimed with dark bitterness. 'We showed you all our resources because we were determined to leave you no excuse. But what could we do against a person who thought in billions where we thought in millions? To you everything was small, unimportant. The full capacity of all our mines was just a drop in the tremendous maw of Earth's metal furnaces. What could we do?'

'Accept the situation!' Thomas shrugged. 'What's the difference whether you sold your metal hereafter to Mars or to Earth; all you ever see are the big freight ships that come here and load up; there would be no objection to making a stipulation that the community have submitted to them the names of governors that Mars would place here, from which they could take their choice. We could also stipulate that the Martians live in separate cities to begin with, and that all business relations between individuals be on a purely voluntary basis; and, oh, a hundred other stipulations could be made, to be effective during, say, the first fifty years.'

'I don't really suppose it matters,' the young man said gloomily. 'I suppose we are stupid fools to object to being handed over like a herd of sheep. It's our pride, and, in a kind of way, I can see your point about the unfairness of the distribution of natural resources. Oh, Lord, here am I talking again. What's the use of you and I arguing on this subject? It's too late. In a few hours that damn thing that's got us sealed in here will wake up and finish us. There's nothing we've got that can hold it back one inch, or one second.'

'Don't be so sure of that!' Thomas said. 'I admit the toughness of this monster has got me worried sick, but don't

28

forget what I've said: These problems have been solved before on other planets.'

'You're mad! I tell you, sir, even with an atomic gun it's touch and go getting the gryb before it gets you. Its hide is so tough it won't begin to disintegrate until your heart's in your boots. What can we do against a thing like that when all we've got is a knife?'

'Let me have the knife,' Thomas replied. 'I want to sharpen it.'

His face twisted into a wry smile. Perhaps it didn't mean much, but the young man had called him 'sir' quite unconsciously. There were psychological implications in the use of the word.

The sustained darkness of that night, the insistent crackle of the palely flickering fire seemed to become more and more alive as the nervous hours twitched by. It was Thomas who was pacing now, his medium-tall, powerful body restless and tense with anxious uncertainty.

It was getting distinctly warmer; the white hoar-frost was melting in places, yielding for the first time to the heat of the spluttering flames; and the chill was no longer reaching clammily through his heated clothes.

A scatter of fine ashes lay on the ground, indication of how completely the fuel had burned away; but even as it was the cave was beginning to show a haze of smoke fumes, through which it was difficult to see properly.

Abruptly there was a great stirring above them; and then a deep, eager mewing, and a scrambling, scratching sound. Ray Bartlett jerked erect from where he had been lying and leaped to his feet. He gasped:

'It's awake, and it's remembered.'

'Well,' said Thomas grimly, 'this is what you've been longing for.'

From across the fire the young man stared at him moodily. He said harshly: 'You don't think I want to die, do you? Besides, I'm beginning to see that killing you will solve nothing. It was a mad scheme.'

'You agree, then,' said Thomas, 'that people who have not rooted themselves into a land, but are simply exploiting it, have no right to expect the living, vital organism of the people to which they belong, to risk a death blow in order to

29

protect them and their purely artificial structure?'

'Oh, I don't know what I think!' Ray Bartlett exclaimed. 'For Heaven's sake, let's quit quibbling. That damned thing –'

A rock bounded down and crashed between them, missing the fire, then vanishing noisily into the darkness beyond. There followed a horrible squeezing, a rasping sound as of brittle scales scraping rock; and then, terribly near, the drumming sound as of a monstrous sledgehammer at work.

'He's breaking off a piece of rock!' Bartlett panted. 'Quick! Get into a concavity against the wall. Those rocks may come tumbling down here, and they won't miss us forever – What are you doing?'

'I'm afraid,' said Thomas in a shaky voice, 'I've got to risk the rock. There's no time to waste.'

His leather-covered hands trembled with the excitement that gripped him as he hastily unfastened one of the glove extensions. He winced a little as his hand emerged into the open air, and immediately jerked it over the hot flame of the fire.

'Phew, it's cold. Must still be about ninety below. I'll have to warm this knife or it'll stick to my skin.'

He held the blade into the flame, finally withdrew it, made a neat incision in the thumb of his bare hand, and wiped the blood on to the knife blade, smearing it on until his hand, blue with the cold, refused to bleed any more. Then he quickly slipped it back into its glove.

It tingled as it warmed, but in spite of the pain he picked up a flaming faggot by its unburned end and walked along into the darkness, his eyes searching the floor. He was vaguely aware of the young man following him.

'Ah,' Thomas said, and even in his own ears his voice sounded wrenched from him. He knelt quiveringly beside a thin crack in the rock. 'This'll be just about right. It's practically against the wall, protected from falling rocks by this projecting edge of wall.'

He glanced up at Bartlett. 'The reason I had us camp here last night instead of farther down was because this ledge is nearly sixty feet long. The gryb is about thirty feet long from tail to snout, isn't it?'

'Yes!'

'Well, this will give it room to come down and walk a few feet; and besides, the cave is wide enough here for us to squeeze past it when it's dead.'

'When it's dead!' the young man echoed with a groan. 'You must be the world's prize fool – '

Thomas scarcely heard him. He was carefully inserting the handle of the knife into the crack of the rock, wedging it in. He tested it.

'Hm-m-m, it seems solid enough. But we'll have to make doubly sure.'

'Hurry!' Bartlett exclaimed. 'We've got to get down to the next level. There's just a chance that there is a connection somewhere below with another cave.'

'There isn't! I went down to investigate while you were sleeping. There are only two more levels after this.'

'For Heaven's sake, man, it'll be here in a minute.'

'A minute is all I need!' Thomas replied, struggling to calm his clamouring heart, to slow the convulsive gasping of his lungs. 'I want to pound these slivers of rock beside the knife to brace it.'

And Thomas pounded, while Bartlett danced frantically from one foot to another in a perfect panic of anxiety. He pounded while that scrambling from above became a roaring confusion, so near now that it was deafening. He pounded while his nerves jangled and shook from the hellish bass mewing that blasted down from the ravenous beast.

And then, with a gasp, he flung aside the piece of rock with which he had been hammering; and the two men lowered themselves recklessly over the ledge – just as two great glowing eyes peered down upon them.

The firelight revealed the vague outlines of a dark, fanged mouth, a thick, twisting tongue; and then there was a scaly glitter as the monstrosity plunged downward right on to the fire.

Thomas saw no more. He let go his hold and skittered downward for nearly twenty feet before he struck bottom. For a minute he lay there, too dizzy to realize that the scrambling noise from above had stopped.

Instead there was a low grunting of pain, and then a sucking sound.

'What the dickens!' Ray Bartlett muttered.

'Wait!' Thomas whispered tensely.

They waited what must have been five minutes, then ten

31

– half an hour. The sucking sound above was weaker. An overtone of wheezing accompanied it, and the grunts had stopped. Once there was a low, hoarse moan of agony.

'Help me up!' Thomas whispered. 'I want to see how close it is to death.'

'Listen,' snapped Ray Bartlett, 'either you're mad or I'm going to be. For Heaven's sake, what's it doing?'

'It smelled the blood on the knife,' Thomas replied, 'and began to lick it. The licking cut its tongue into ribbons, which whipped it into a frenzy, because with every lick more of its own blood would flow into its mouth. You say it loves blood. For the last half-hour it's been gorging itself on its own blood. Primitive stuff, common to all the planets. Civilized men, apparently, never think of things like that.'

'I guess,' Ray Bartlett said in a queer voice after a long moment, 'there's nothing now to prevent us getting back to the Five Cities.'

Thomas stared with narrowed eyes at the other's vague bulk in the darkness. 'Nothing, except – you!'

They climbed in silence to where the gryb lay dead. Thomas was aware of Barltett watching him as he gingerly removed the knife from where it was wedged into the rock. Then abruptly, harshly, Bartlett said:

'Give me that!'

Thomas hesitated, then handed the knife over. It was possible he would have to take the terrific risk of telling young Bartlett the truth about this whole business. For undoubtedly the younger man was once again all enemy.

Outside, the morning greeted them, bleak, yet somehow more inviting. The little red Sun was well above the horizon, and something else was in the sky, too: a huge red ball of pale fire, Jupiter the giant sinking now towards the western horizon.

The sky, the world of Europa, was lighter, brighter; even the rocks didn't look so dead, nor so black. A strong wind was blowing; and it added to the sense of life. The morning seemed cheerful after the black night, as if hope was once again possible.

'It's a false hope,' thought Thomas. 'The Lord save me from the stubborn duty sense of an honest man. He's going to attack.'

Yet the fury of attack, when it came, surpassed his expectations. He caught the movement, the flash of the knife out of the corner of his eye – and whipped aside.

The knife caught the resisting fabric of the arm of his electrically heated suit, scraped a foot-long scar on that obstinate, half-metallic substance, and then Thomas was dancing away along a ledge of firm rock.

'You . . . silly . . . fool!' he gasped. 'You don't know what you're doing.'

'You bet I know!' Bartlett ground out. 'I've got orders to kill you, and I'm going to in spite of your silver tongue. You're the devil himself for talking, but now you die.'

He leaped forward, knife poised, and Thomas let him come. There was a way of disarming a man with a knife, provided the man did not know the method and provided it worked the first time.

Bartlett grunted as he leaped; his free hand grabbed at Thomas, and that was all Thomas needed. Just a damned amateur who didn't know knife fighters didn't try for holds.

Thomas snatched at the clawlike spread of that striking hand, caught it with grim strength and jerked the young man past him with every ounce of his power. As Bartlett shot by him, propelled by his own momentum as well as by that arm-wrenching pull, Thomas twisted along with him. At the last instant he braced himself for the shock and sent the two-hundred-pound body spinning along like a top.

Frantically, Ray Bartlett fought for balance. But there was no mercy in that rough ground. Upjutting rock snagged his feet; he fell with mind-stunning violence, kicked weakly and lay still.

Thomas picked up the knife from where it had fallen.

'I'll keep this,' he said when the other's glazed eyes began to show animation. 'But what am I going to do with you? We've got twelve days, at least, during which I'll be at your mercy a score of times a day. A swiftly heaved rock to smash my head, a sudden shove as we skirt some crater – '

'I'll . . . do . . . it . . . too.'

Thomas frowned. 'At least, you're honest. That makes it possible for me not to kill you, but to trust you with a secret so important that if the barest hint of it got out in advance it would shatter the greatest diplomatic stroke of the ages. But I must have your most sacred word of honour that not one word will escape you under any circumstances.'

'I guess I can promise that!' Ray Bartlett said in a thick, unsteady voice; then, with more fire: 'But I'll see you in hell before I change my mind.'

'You promise, nevertheless.'

'Yes, I promise, but there's nothing –'

Thomas cut him short: 'There has never been a more enlightened group of men on Mars than the present government. If we hand over Europa to prove our good will to the doubters among the opposition, that government will, immediately on re-election, vote to join the Earth-Venus union. I need hardly tell you that the thing is so tremendous that it staggers the imagination. For the first time in the history of men –'

'Suppose they lose the election?'

'We can trust that crew of rabble-rousers to encroach immediately on the rights of the Europans, as defined by the agreement we will draw up. Whereupon we shall declare the agreement null and void and take over Europa.'

'Bah! That means war, and you wouldn't have the nerve.'

Thomas's steely eyes gazed unflinchingly at the younger man. 'Let me tell you that I am the dominating minister in the present Earth-Venus government; and I hope I have convinced you that fear is not one of my characteristics. My colleagues and I do not fear, but hate, war. However, we are convinced that war will not be necessary. The government on Mars will win the election; and I think that you agree with me there.'

Bartlett muttered: 'Getting Europa handed to them on a platter ought to swing any election, I guess.'

Thomas ignored his surliness, and in a voice that was queerly husky he said: 'I have talked of repetition being a rule of life. But somewhere along the pathway of the Universe there must be a first time for everything, a first peaceful solution along sound sociological lines of the antagonisms of great sovereign powers.

'Some day man will reach the stars, and all the old, old problems will repeat themselves. When that day comes, we must have established sanity in the very souls of men, so firmly rooted that there will be an endless repetition of peaceful solutions.'

He stood up. 'Think it over, and then decide for yourself whether you've got the nerve to face the recriminations of your friends for letting me come in alive. There's a dark, bitter period ahead of Europa, and the agony of your people will be heaped on your head. It's a hard choice.'

In the west, mighty Jupiter was being engulfed by the blue, dark horizon, an age-old cycle repeating. The strong wind died, and there was quiet upon that wild, fantastic land. Thomas was aware of the young man walking behind him – too aware; it made him less alert for what was ahead.

Abruptly he stumbled to the edge of a jagged black hole that fell away into sheer, dreadful depths. He hung there, teetering, frantic, over the abyss.

And then two iron-hard hands caught his shoulder, jerked him back from that desperate danger.

'Be careful, sir!' breathed the anxious voice of Ray Bartlett. 'Be careful, or you'll be killed.'

HUMANS, GO HOME

Chapter I

'Each morning,' Miliss said, 'is the dawn of nothing.'

So she was leaving.

'No children, no future,' the woman continued. 'Every day like every other, going nowhere. The sun shines, but I'm in darkness – '

It was, Dav realized, the beginning of the death talk. He tensed his perfect muscles. His blue eyes – they could observe with a deep understanding on many levels – misted with sudden anxiety. But his lips and his infinitely adaptable tongue – which in its time, and that time was long indeed, had spoken a hundred languages – said no word.

He watched her, made no move to help her and no effort to stop her as she piled her clothes on to a powered dolly, to be wheeled into the east wing of the house. Her clothes, her jewels from a score of planets; her special pillows and other bedroom articles; the specific furniture – each piece a jewel in itself – in which she stored her possessions; her keys – plain and electronic, pushbotton-control types for energy relays and tiny combination systems for entry into the great Reservoir of the Symbols – all now were made ready to be transported with a visibly growing impatience.

Finally she snapped, 'Where is your courtesy? Where is your manliness – letting a woman do all this work?'

Dav said evenly, 'It would be foolish of me to help you leave me.'

'So all those years of politeness – I merely bought them with unalienated behaviour. You have no natural respect for a woman – or for me.'

She yelled the accusations at him. Dav felt a tremor stir inside him, not from her words but from the meaning of the anger that accompanied them, the unthinking automatic quality of that anger.

He said flatly, 'I am not going to help you leave me.'

It was the kind of answer one made to a stereotype. His hope had to be that these preliminaries of the death compulsion could be headed off.

His words, however, were far from effective. Her blonde cheeks gradually turned to a darker colour as the day – unlike other days, which were often as slow as forever – devoured itself, digesting hours in great gulps. And still her possessions, more numerous evidently than she had realized, were not shifted from the west to the east wing of the long, big house.

Late in the afternoon Dav pointed out that her act of withdrawal was a well-known phenomenon of internal female chemistry. He merely wanted from her the analytical consciousness of this fact – and her permission to give her the drugs that would rectify the condition.

She rejected the argument. From her lips poured a stream of angry rationalizations.

'The woman is always to blame. The fault is in her, not in the man. The things that I have had to put up with – they don't count – '

Long ago, when she was still in her natural state, before the administration of the first immortality injections, there might have been genuine cause for accusations which attacked male subjectiveness. But that was back in a distant time. After the body had been given chemical aids, all things were balanced by a diet of understanding drugs.

Dav located the relevant book in the library and abandoned his initial attempts to keep from her the seriousness of her condition. He walked beside her and read paragraphs detailing the emotional affliction that had led to the virtual destruction of the human race. The dark thoughts she had expressed – and was now acting on – were described so exactly that abruptly, as he walked beside her, he bent in her direction and held the book up to her face. His finger pointed out the significant sentences.

Miliss stopped. Her eyes, a deceptive grey-green, narrowed. Her lips tightly compressed, unmistakably resisting what he was doing. Yet she spoke in a mild tone.

'Let me see that.'

She reached for the book.

Dav surrendered it reluctantly. The sly purpose he detected in her seemed even more automatic than the earlier anger. In those few hours she appeared to have become a simpler, more primitive person.

So he was not surprised when she raised the book above her head and, with a wordless vocalization, flung it to the floor behind him.

They had come to within a few yards of a door which led to her part of the house. Dav resignedly stooped to pick up the book, aware of her walking rapidly to that door. It opened and slammed shut behind her.

After silence descended, after the coming of the brilliant, purple Jana twilight, when the sun finally sank out of sight behind the slickrock mountains to the west and the sweet, soft darkness of the shining, starlit night of Jana settled, Dav tested the connecting doors between the two wings. All four resisted his pull with the rigidity of unbreakable locks.

The following morning.

The sound of a buzzer precipitated Dav into the new day. For a meagre moment the hope stirred in him that Miliss was calling. But he rejected that possibility even as he formed the image in his mind that triggered the nearest thought amplifier. His dismissal of the idea turned out to be correct. The buzzing ceased. A picture formed on the ceiling screen. It showed a Jana tradesboy with groceries standing at the outer door.

Dav spoke to the boy in the Jana tongue and glided out of bed. Presently he was accepting the bag from the long-nosed youth, who said, 'There was a message to bring this to another part of the house. But I didn't understand clearly – '

Dav hesitated with the fleeting realization that the ever-present Java spy system was probably behind those words. And that if he explained, the information would be instantly relayed to the authorities. Not that he could ever tell these beings the truth. Their time for immortality was not yet.

Nor was it their time to learn the numerous details of the final disaster – when, in a period of a few months, virtually the entire human population of the galaxy rejected life, refused the prolongation drugs. People by the billion hid themselves and died unattended and uncaring.

A few, of course, were captured by appalled survivors and

38

had treatment forced on them. A wrong solution, it developed. For the people who sympathized and helped, by those very desperate feelings, in some manner attuned themselves into the same deadly psychic state as the naturally doomed.

In the end it was established that the only real survivors were individuals who felt a scathing contempt for people who could not be persuaded to accept help. Such a disdainful survivor could sarcastically argue with someone – yes, for a while. But force him, no.

Dav stood at the door of the great house in which he and Miliss had lived these several hundred years. And he realized that his was the moment.

To save himself, he had to remember that what Miliss was doing deserved his total disgust.

He shrugged and said, 'My wife has left me. She is living alone on the other side of the house. So deliver these to the door at the far east side.'

He thrust the bag of groceries back into the hands of the Jana and motioned him away.

The boy took the big sack and backed off with visible reluctance.

'Your wife has left you?' he echoed finally.

Dav nodded. In spite of himself he felt vaguely regretful at the revelation. To these Jana males, pursuit of females began early and continued into late life, terminating approximately at the moment of death. Until now the human woman had been a forbidden and unapproachable female. But no question – there had always been a perverted Jana male interest in Miliss.

With an abrupt dismissal Dav suppressed such thoughts. What they represented was unimportant. It did not matter.

Later that day he saw her in her part of the garden, lissome, still beautiful, showing no signs of immediate deterioration. Apparently – even on this second day – she was still an immortal blonde woman. Seeing her, Dav shrugged and turned away, his lip curling, and in his mind the thought that she was not really human.

She could not reason.

Still later, darkness had fallen when, after testing with the various keys the Blaze Points of the Great Reservoir of the Symbols, he came to the summit of the hill from which he could see their long, white house.

Its night lights showed the garden and the glint of the river on the far side. But around it nothing moved. Silent stood the old house, familiar, a centuries-old landmark.

Something about the stillness below disturbed him. He had a sudden feeling that no one was there. The house itself was dark – both wings.

Puzzled but not alarmed – because he was safe and Miliss did not count, for she was doomed anyway – Dav hurried down. He tried first a door to her wing. It was unlocked.

An amplified thought hit him. Miliss speaking mentally.

Dav, I have been arrested by Jaer Dorrish and am being taken to a military prison. I have the impression that this is a Dorrish clan takeover scheme and that it is connected with the fact that Rocquel has now been gone for a year. That's all . . .

The account was succinct, as impersonal as his own receipt of it. She had left him a communication of facts. In her message was no appeal, no request for help.

Dav stood silent. He was evoking a mental picture of the sardonic Jaer Dorrish and, more vaguely, the image of Rocquel, the hereditary leader of the Janae, who had disappeared slightly more than one Jana year ago. A year on Jana was three hundred ninety-two and a fraction days long.

He felt opposed to Jaer, of course – in a way wished the steely-minded Rocquel were back. Usurpations usually meant trouble and unrest. But if it had to be, it had to. The Janae constituted a problem for him as Guardian of the Symbols. But individuals among them were not, in one sense, important. Though he had liked Rocquel, and still liked Rocquel's – widow?

Nerda.

In the morning, I'll look into this . . .

Chapter II

Rocquel's senses blurred in arriving. He lay down for a few seconds on the shadowy grass. It was already day – fairly early morning; he noticed when he climbed to his feet. He could see the palace, visible among the trees of the vast garden which surrounded the building.

Rocquel stood for a moment, head thrown back, breathing deeply of the air of his native planet. A year had seemed a long absence. So much had happened. Yet the sky of Jana and these hills that he had known in his lost youth so intimately seemed unchanged. Here, during all those tremendous days of his absence, time had sculptured with a slow and exacting chisel. A gentle wind blew in Rocquel's face as he started slowly towards the road beyond the near trees, the winding road that would take him to the palace.

Incredibly, he made it to within a hundred yards of the sprawl of building before a Jana male came suddenly from around some trees, saw him, and stopped. Rocquel recognized the other at once; Jaer Dorrish. Jaer was a big fellow, bigger than Rocquel, good-looking in a swarthy way. His eyes narrowed. He seemed to brace himself.

He said arrogantly in the tone of one addressing an intruder, 'What are you doing here – stranger?'

Rocquel walked forward at a deliberate pace. He had been cautioned to take up his old position before he revealed the new facets of his personality. He didn't need the warning – it was implicit in the sly act of a person who knew him, pretending not to.

The problem of what one of the Dorrish men was doing in the Rocquel grounds so early in the morning – or ever – he would come to later. Right now the denial of his idenity was surpassingly significant.

This time Jaer Dorrish showed his understanding of the situation.

'By Dilit,' he said exultantly, 'I've caught you unarmed.'

He drew his sword in a single, continuous movement and began to circle Rocquel, apparently not quite believing that he need merely rush in and slash. His eyes speculatively sized up Rocquel's condition.

Rocquel backed and simultaneously turned. He paused where Jaer had been standing. It took him moments to locate consciously the symbol made by the invisible Tizane energy, which he had directed to the spot the instant he saw Jaer. He kicked it cautiously, leaning backward so that his body would not be attracted by the symbol. His foot tingled unpleasantly – it was a feeling of something grabbing at him, something very powerful that did not quite reach him but

41

only clawed the outer threads of his clothing, failing to get a good hold. Twice he pulled clear of it. Presently he was able to step over the broken ground without experiencing a reaction.

He was already out of danger when Jaer laughed and replaced his sword.

The big male said arrogantly, 'If one does not threaten, one cannot show mercy. You see, Rocquel, I expected that you would return today. I have had observers watching the grounds all night so that I could have this confrontation with you.' He grimaced triumphantly. 'I analyse that you owe your return to me. Because yesterday I arrested the human woman, Miliss, and here you are this morning, exactly as I anticipated. It was a sudden intuition of mind. You have a lot of explaining to do – sir.'

Jaer was visibly jubilant. He waved at somebody behind Rocquel. Rocquel was wary of the gesture. In his careful defensive manoeuvring he had gotten his back to the buildings. Finally he glanced carefully around and saw that Nerda was walking towards them.

As she came near, she said, 'You were not really in danger were you? It showed in your manner.'

Rocquel said, 'Not from one person.'

He walked to her, and she did not resist his kiss. She might as well have. Her lips were cool and unresponsive. Her passive body did not welcome his embrace.

Rocquel drew back, scowling. An old anger against this defiant young female rose to gall him.

'Damn you,' he said. 'Aren't you glad to see me?'

Nerda merely gazed at him cooly.

'I forgot,' said Rocquel, stung. 'It was a welcome period of rest for you. It's difficult for a male to remember that Jana females do not have feelings.'

His wife shrugged.

Rocquel stared at her, curious now rather than hostile. Like all Jana females, she was icily aloof. He had married her in the usual fashion by having her father bring her to his house. She had subsequently born him a son and a daughter, but in the Jana female tradition she continued to treat him like an intruder in her life – whom she must tolerate but did not particularly care to have around.

Rocquel scowled jealously.

'What about Jaer?'

That brought a reply.

'I think he has already explained his presence. Rather than have any further words from him, I would prefer to hear your explanation of your absence.'

Rocquel rejected explanations. 'Come along,' he said gruffly. 'Let us go inside.'

There were things to do. The news of his return would spread rapidly. The men in control of the council must not be allowed too much time to decide what to do about him. There would be regents, generals, and their aides – who would be unhappy at the return of the hereditary ruler of the army. Before this night he must again be recognized as entitled by law and right to wield the sceptre of his sphere.

He took Nerda's arm gently. The move was calculated. He wanted to enter the palace beside her, his identity given validity by her presence. A year was a long time on Jana. Jana males particularly had short memories. He could not have planned his arrival better if he had personally made all the arrangements in advance.

Rocquel had the tocsin sounded as soon as he reached the main guard station. Shortly the palace guard and the servants were drawn up in five lines of a hundred each. He addressed them in his deepest baritone, recalling himself to the older men, inviting the younger men to remember his face and body structure. He wanted them to be able to identify him under all circumstances.

He felt a little better when that job was done and the people had been dismissed to return to their duties. But not much better. The servants and guards could be talked to like a schoolroom full of children. But not the officers. Not the nobility.

He had a new, superior – yet not at all condescending – attitude toward these people. They were simple souls. He now understood how rapidly Dav and Miliss were rushing Janae into civilization by a trial-and-error system that attempted to take each man for what he was.

The lower classes were given easy tests. Those who showed even a modicum of mechanical ability were soon placed on assembly lines, where they performed one action, then two, then several – but never many. For decades now some pretty sharp mechanics had been coming up the line, and from their ranks arose a new class – engineers.

The officers and nobility were a different breed. Quick to take insult, they were truly impervious to all but the barest elements of education. They had been persuaded that being able to read and write was a mark of distinction, but they were never entirely convinced. Why, they wanted to know grimly, were the lower classes also being taught reading and writing? The resultant, infinitely stubborn attitude had made it necessary to have a different written language for the people – one the upper classes didn't respect – before the nobles sullenly allowed their children to go to special, separate schools.

Telling the nobility of his return, it seemed to Rocquel, would have to be done at an all-male dinner in the vast dining hall adjoining the even vaster jousting room.

About mid-morning Dav at last felt free to put through a call to Nerda. There was a long delay. Finally an aide came to the phone.

He said in a formal tone. 'The queen wishes me to inform you that her lord, Rocquel, has returned, and since he will in future represent the power of the armed forces, her talking to you might be misconstrued at this stage. That is all, sir.'

Dav hung up, startled. The great Rocquel was home. Where had he been?

The hereditary general had always been a male first, his every movement and the tenor of his being expressing the quiescent violence of his powerful, supermasculine breed. It seemed an unfortunate coincidence for Miliss that the deadly, narrow-eyed Jana ruler had returned. Dav divined that, if a struggle for power took place, Miliss might be its first victim.

After some thought, Dav phoned the palace a second time and asked for Rocquel.

Once more he endured delay.

At last another aide said, 'His Excellency, the lord-general Rocquel wishes me to inform you that a new law will be promulgated tomorrow to the council. He invites you to attend the council meeting which will be held at the slickrock rendezvous.'

*

The dinner that night shocked Rocquel. He had forgotten the extreme coarseness of his peers – at least it had become vague in his mind. An uproar of yelling and jesting began as the first male arrived. More arrivals simply added to the pandemonium. Things quieted down only to a degree when the meal was finally served. Plates clanked. Forks and knives clattered. Males yelled a peculiar type of acceptable insult at acquaintances farther along a table – insults having to do with the jester's belief that the other lacked sexual prowess. Such remarks always brought bellows of laughter, while onlookers insultingly urged the object of the attack to prove his capabilities.

Yet since humour always probed the abyss of a male's sensitivity to criticism, suddenly a word would be unacceptable. In a flash the aggrieved male was on his feet, ragefully demanding satisfaction. Moments later the two nobles, yelling furiously at each other, would stamp out to the jousting room and add the clash of their steel to the sound of the dozens that were already there.

Shortly a scream of outrage announced the first blood had been drawn. In the presence of Rocquel the custom was that the male initially blooded in any way was expected to acknowledge defeat. Such acknowledgement meant that the insult was nullified. But the loser who felt himself still aggrieved could demand a later reckoning away from the palace grounds.

It was of this assembled group of mad creatures that Rocquel demanded silence when the eating was completed. Getting it, he gave the explanation for his absence that had been suggested to him – a religious withdrawal, a year of wandering among the people as a mendicant, a time of self-searching and thorough selflessness, of deliberate, temporary abdication of power.

He concluded his fabricated account.

'I saw our people in their daily actions. I lived among them, survived on their generosity, and can report that the Jana world is indeed a worthy one.'

He received a prolonged ovation. But a bad moment came when he presently went into the jousting room, where the guests had drifted after his talk.

A voice grated beside his ear, 'Your sword, sire.'

Rocquel experienced a blank instant as he realized he was

being challenged.

He swung around as of old in a swift, automatic defence action. His blade came out, weaving, before he saw that his challenger was Jaer Dorrish.

Rocquel poised, sword ready. He gazed questioningly into the dark, cynical eyes of his enemy.

From somewhere in the sea of faces surrounding them, from out of the diminishing curtain of sound – diminishing as more males grew aware of what was happening – Rocquel was aware of a top officer speaking sharply.

'Jaer – have you forgotten? You have to state your reason when you challenge the crown. And it must be a reason acceptable to the majority present.'

'My reason,' said Jaer in his deliberate fashion, 'is that story of where he said he was during the past year – '

The officer who had spoken walked forward. He was grave, fortyish, narrow-eyed.

'Is it a matter of misunderstanding the story or of rejecting it?'

Silence had settled over the room, and the words made an echo into the distances of that cavernous space. The question visibly gave Jaer pause. His expression showed his comprehension that a to-the-death had to follow any total challenge of a noble's word.

Abruptly he laughed and put away his sword.

He said, 'I think I shall ask privately for a clarification. If Rocquel decides what I have to say is truly a reason for a challenge – then we shall have our bout. Perhaps tomorrow.' He thereupon stepped close to Rocquel and said in a low, insolent voice. 'Your Excellency – the coincidence of my arresting Miliss and your prompt return needs to be explained. If the two are not related – you will, of course, have no objection to my plans for disposing of her.'

Rocquel said evenly, 'If you are operating within the frame of the law – '

'The law is what the council decides,' replied Jaer arrogantly. 'Do I have your word that you will not interfere – in view of my suspicions?'

'There will be a new law,' said Rocquel in a formal tone. 'Within the frame of that law – I shall not interfere.'

He walked away, leaving Jaer Dorrish with a black scowl on his face and a query about the 'new law' unspoken on his pursed lips. In his mind Rocquel read the thought that this very night he must attend on the human woman – must force her before any protecting law was passed.

Yet Rocquel could not be sure he had read correctly even when Jaer left the party within minutes.

Nerda was waiting for Rocquel when he came in. He was late, very late. As soon as he entered – and after he had nodded to her – she retreated to her dressing-room and began to get ready for bed. He watched her shadow through the translucent door. A regretful thought passed through his mind that he should have given her permission to retire without waiting for his return.

Presently he rejected the thought of such leniency. According to Jana law a wife could not undress at night to go to bed until her husband gave permission. She could lie down with her clothes on. She could even sleep, though that was frowned on. She could go to bed before his return only with his written permission or if a doctor stated in writing or in the presence of witnesses that she was ill.

The rules seemed harsh. But Rocquel had read the ancient documents containing the results of studies made of Jana female behaviour prior to the passing of the stringent laws, and there was no question. Jana females would associate with males only when forced. A female, unforced, would promptly move off by herself and remain that way all her life.

The facts had been set down by amazed historians who named names and places. The truths of the long-ago experiments in allowing freedom to females were attested to by famous people of Jana history. There was no point in repeating the experience in modern times.

Jana females had no maternal instinct and particularly detested their male children. It had been a sad thing to read some of the comments made by females during the free period.

A male child will eventually become a Jana male – that most detestable being. And so any charming childlike attributes he may have are an illusion . . .

Another female had been in favour of the race's dying out – because its continuance required that Jana males also survive, to which she was 'totally opposed.'

47

What could males do, confronted by such females?
They had done it.

The laws were just and as kind as they could be. A female could complain if she suffered any ill-treatment – and receive an immediate hearing from a court. No expense was spared by the State to protect her from a brutal husband.

In return she must do her duty by her husband and her children. Since she had no feeling about her functions, the law prescribed her exact routine.

Obviously even the hereditary general could not lightly alter either the custom or the law. Nerda came to bed, and presently he gave her permission to sleep.

She slept – it seemed, instantly.

Chapter III

Miliss heard a key in the lock of her cell. She had not undressed. She sat up in the rough bunk and watched curiously as a manlike figure, waving a long flashlight, unlocked the door and entered.

From the vast shadowy size of him she divined his identity. But not until he deliberately raised the light and beamed it into his face did she recognize Jaer Dorrish.

His face, like that of all Jana males, was too long, too much given over to nose. But the skin was a clear reddish colour and smooth.

She was not repelled.

At least, she thought, the Janae were a distinctly human-like breed, for which – in view of the fate she sensed was in store of her – she was thankful. It did not occur to her to formulate in her mind the mental pattern that would activate a thought amplifier in the house where she and Dav lived – no help for her from that rigid mind, she decided.

But she did have purpose of her own, adaptable to this situation. It had been growing on her all day. The male stepped briskly across the cell towards her cot.

She said hurriedly, 'I've been thinking about what you told me last night – your prediction that Rocquel would return as a consequence of my arrest. And it happened. He did come back.'

Jaer stopped his forward movement. He did not reply. Her next words quivered on the tip of her tongue but remained unspoken.

Miliss was startled. She had an enormous sensitivity to small signals. He had been coming forward with that Jana-male arrogance, his whole manner vibrating with the message that he would not be denied.

And now he stood still. And the way he stood telegraphed uncertainty.

'Is something wrong?' Miliss asked.

More silence, a sense of darker emotions. She was astounded. Jana males were reputed to have a peculiar calm humour in the rape situation. Both humour and *savoir faire* required expression in words, not silence.

During the strange pause, like a suspension of time in the cell, she had nevertheless become aware of the night and the prison. A time had been on Jana when there had been no prisons, only a few compounds where 'enemies' were kept prior to execution.

On Jana, for more millennia than she cared to recall, people had been tolerated – or executed. No middle situation had existed. This and similar prisons were actually a great victory for less harsh attitudes.

So the sounds of a vast life around her were presently heartening to Miliss. She heard metallic clanks, distant throat raspings, Jana males snarling in their sleep, and occasional echoes of faraway voices. Sounds of many prisoners. The Nunbrid prison was large. It was filled with people who would be tried in court for their offences and who were not subject – as had once been the case – to the compulsive masculine rage of some intolerant noble.

A feeling of peaceful accomplishment was settling over Miliss. Dav and she had civilized these people.

Jaer finally spoke.

'I had a sudden insight – and I'm having another one.'

His voice was strained, not really calm. She sensed in its tone an advantage for her. Somehow the situation was no longer as dangerous as it had been. This male was genuinely disturbed.

By what?

Miliss pressed her own purpose upon him.

49

'Is that all you can say about the coincidence of your prediction and Rocquel's return?'

'I'm still wondering about it myself,' was the grim answer.

The threat was in his voice again. She rushed past it.

'Don't you realize the impossibility of such an unsupported insight – the odds against its baring truth?'

For a tense moment in the unyielding closeness of the cell, in the darkness broken only by a flashlight that sometimes pointed at her and sometimes at the metal bars – and occasionally, briefly, at Jaer himself – she thought that he would acknowledge reason and dismiss the subject. But Jana nobles, she shortly decided in despair, were not up to her kind of strict logic. His mien told her he was accepting his intuition.

For a long moment, while he stood there silently, her fear grew.

Then: 'There's only one explanation,' he said slowly. 'Rocquel was in hiding with you and Dav while he was gone.'

'No. That's absolutely not true. If you're acting on that assumption – you're in danger.'

'Danger?'

'There's a hidden force at work. It can strike at you if you ignore it. In fact, it probably has already struck – or how could you have had two insights?'

'You're trying to alarm me,' said Jaer harshly. 'And a Jana male cannot be frightened.'

'But he can think about how best to survive,' countered Miliss. 'At least' – she couldn't help the biting remark – 'the males I know always do.'

Again silence filled the cell. The light winked off. Into that darkness and that silence Miliss projected what seemed to her to be the only possible explanation.

'What has happened means that you've been programmed,' she said.

'Programmed? I don't understand.'

'It's impossible that you could have a second major intuition unless somebody had installed it in your mind under mechanical hypnosis.'

'I just had it. It's my own thought.'

'It's not your own thought. You're being manipulated.' She broke off. 'Don't you see, you couldn't possibly – being

50

a Jana noble – have all by yourself predicted Rocquel's return on the basis of my arrest. It's too radical and fantastic a prediction. Yet it came true. And now another one? Impossible.'

Once more he was silent. The flashlight was on again, its beam tilted casually, showing his scowling face, narrowed eyes and lower lip pushed up. He was evidently having unpleasant, calculating thoughts.

Abruptly he asked, 'Why did you and Dav separate?'

Miliss hesitated, then said, 'He was more and more adopting the attitudes and behaviour of the Jana male – and treating me as Jana males treat Jana females. I had had enough years ago – but we were alone here, two human beings, the last of our kind in this area. So I tried to make my peace with the situation as Jana females have done for so long.'

There was actually more to it than that. It had, of course, kept occuring to her that the frequent despair she had felt over Dav might in fact be the death wish that had destroyed the human race. She had fought against her growing embitterment, until, one day not too long since, she had had an insight of her own.

Human males were, had always been, exactly as vicious as the Janae. But human women, having their own maternal instinct to satisfy, had endlessly compromised with the egotistical villains. The need for motherhood had put a fortunate – for the men and the race – veil over a woman's awareness of the impossible true nature of the beasts.

Once she had recognized the thought, leaving Dav was only a matter of a brief period of rethinking her reasons, and convincing herself finally.

Jaer's voice came grimly.

He said, 'I didn't have my first insight until after I had arrested you. I've had my second one in your presence. So you're doing this to me. By Dilit, woman – '

Miliss said urgently, 'Tell me what your second insight is.'

When he had told her, she said, 'But that's ridiculous – what good does that do me?'

Jaer must have recognized her logic. He stood very still.

After a long pause he said slowly, 'But I did get both thoughts in your presence, so someone knows I'm here.'

His manner showed unease. The implication of danger was visibly penetrating his awareness. Miliss sensed her advantage.

She said, 'What is so meaningless about these insights is that I detect that your purpose in arresting me was entirely personal. You saw a possibility of challenging the throne and simultaneously obtaining me as a mistress – '

'Silence, woman.' Jaer sounded alarmed. 'I have never desired the throne – that's treason. I'd better leave before I damage you and ruin my case against you in court. But don't think I'm through with you.'

The light winked out. Quick steps sounded. A metal door clicked open and clanged shut.

She heard him retreating along a corridor. And realized that she was almost as shaken as he.

That second insight, she told herself, *is absolutely mad . . .*

But for the first time in many years she slept poorly.

Chapter IV

The next day.

Shortly after sunrise the council members began cycling up to the meeting place at the beginning of the slickrock range, seven miles west of Nunbrid. By the time Rocquel arrived on his new motorbike, Dav and eight Jana males of high rank were already there. The human sat on his bike off to one side, but the Jana nobles were impatiently gunning their motors, visibly anxious to get started on their hazardous meeting-in-motion.

Rocquel was greeted by a number of insulting but quite good-natured comments about his overweight machine. He responded with well-placed sneers about overcautious small-bike riders. But he was curious. There had been changes in design during his absence. Wheeling around with the casual daring of an expert cyclist, he made quick, searching examination of the mount of each council member to see what time and manufacturers had wrought.

As always for slickrocking, all the motorcycles were small, tough, and light. But Rocquel noticed that three of the bikes were smaller than he remembered – not more than 100 cc, perhaps even 90 or 80 – compared to his 175-cc machine.

He questioned the three owners about it. He was still getting boastful replies when Jaer Dorrish and a sly-eyed air-force officer roared up and charged their metal steeds up the first incline.

Jaer yelled, 'Meeting called to order – '

A number of nobles uttered wild cries, gunned their motors, and took off in pursuit of the late-comers.

Dav brought up the rear.

Moments later everyone was in motion, and the meeting of the supreme council of Jana was in session.

In the old days – before the machines – a king had held his council meetings while riding a tamed, high-backed Mesto-beast. The Mestos were dangerous, cunning creatures, always looking for an opportunity to upset their riders, and Mesto-riding was, accordingly, considered great fun. But a Mesto simply could not cover the distances or go over the rough and beautiful slickrock country.

At first the nobles climbed steadily, strung out unevenly, bobbing up and down over domes, knobs, and ridges, skipping at a good clip over the almost glass-smooth, steel-hard straights. Rocquel, coming up from behind, kept edging up to Jaer and finally had his bike racing along parallel to the bright green machine of the big male.

'What's on the agenda?' he yelled.

Jaer's answering cry brought up the subject of Miliss. He made a slashing gesture with one hand, cutting the air with it as if it were a blade, then showed his teeth in a grimacing smile.

He shouted, 'I propose that this woman be put to death.'

'On what grounds?' Rocquel roared back, surprised.

Jaer's suggestion was discourteous in view of the fact that Dav was at the council meeting. Or was it possible that Jaer had not yet seen Dav?

As the day dragged by, Jaer's unawareness of Dav began to seem less and less a coincidence. But Jaer's intentness on Miliss and on the new law might have accounted for his attitude towards Dav.

Dav anticipated a crisis as soon as he was told what was on the agenda, and the nature of the new law.

The law itself required no special explanation for him. It was he who had proposed the idea of a constitutional monarchy to a resistant Rocquel. The very next day – a year ago – the powerful Jana leader had gone off on a religious hegira.

Now he was back, acceptant.

Mentally, Dav triggered a thought amplifier. It in turn channelled power into a relay that blazed one of the Symbols.

The Symbol of a constitutional monarchy.

That done, he considered with mirthless good humour the proposal to execute Miliss. Ironic that Jaer was planning to put on trial a person already doomed.

Should Jaer be told?

But when Dav finally joined the group, the crisis came so rapidly that there was no time to mention anything.

The council members stopped in front of a big cave, at the 9000-foot level. Here the great nobles of Jana sat on bikes with engines idling while they gulped breakfast.

Rocquel was aware of an ugly, throaty sound from Jaer. He spun around and saw Dav easing his bike into the clearing. Dav came to a full stop.

Beside Rocquel, Jaer let out a bellow and gunned his motor.

That night Rocquel described the day to Nerda, then asked curiously, 'What do you think happened to Jaer? You know more about what Dav can do than anyone.'

Conversations between them were not common. She was not required by law or custom to speak to him as long as she performed her wifely duties. He was not surprised when she did not reply. But he deduced from the thoughtful expression on her face that she was considering the matter and would eventually give him an answer.

Yet it was morning before she answered.

'A symbol,' she said then, 'as Dav has described it, represents a real thing or thought. It is not itself the thing or the thought – '

Rocquel waited, uneasily aware that he was being presented with a concept that might be too subtle for a Jana noble – too subtle even for himself, despite his past year of indoctrination.

Nerda continued, 'When the Symbol representing constitutional monarchy is finally a part of the thinking of millions of Janae, the force of it in all those minds will maintain such a system for decades under normal circumstances – or at least until another Symbol replaces it, which, of course, is happening very rapidly with Dav and Miliss forcing us into civilization.'

Rocquel felt helpless before her explanation. She seemed to understand what she was saying, and he didn't.

We males of the nobility are really no longer a part of what is happening . . .

It was discouraging, but he persisted.

'What I saw,' he said, 'was Jaer's motorcycle stop – not short – but as if it ran into an elastic wall that took the full force of his forward impetus and gently flung him back. He ended up on the ground. But he was not hurt.'

'He struck the Symbol,' said Nerda. 'These Symbols have become progressively more violent in their reaction. The most violent so far is the Symbol of a constitutional monarchy.'

He said, 'You say the Symbol. But what was the force involved?'

'The force of the Symbol.' Her expression showed her awareness of his bewilderment. 'Don't you see?' she urged. 'All those millions of people who believe.'

What Rocquel was seeing was that he had made a mistake in asking her for her opinion. He wanted to say that nobody yet believed in the new law. It would not even be publicly announced until later this morning. But his awful feeling leaped past that idea to the more personal awareness that he had lowered himself in her eyes. He recalled with a sinking sensation the Jana-male conviction that if a female even once gained a genuine advantage over her husband, it was the end of their relationship. Nothing the male did after that could repair the damage.

Fighting for recovery, he nodded and said aloud, 'I see. Your many conversations with Dav have been very educational and valuable for both of us. I congratulate you. It's a difficult concept.'

He divined from an odd look in her eyes that she saw through his verbal stratagem.

She said slowly, 'We mustn't expect too muct from a constitutional monarchy in terms of change in the passions. Rule of law merely regulates a society in a more orderly fashion than absolutism. An accused individual is no longer subject to arbitrary judgements but is allowed time by the courts to defend himself within the frame of the law. Yet in the end he may pay the same penalty.' She concluded: 'And so, to answer your question of last night – I believe we shall see how Jaer was affected by the way he allows the trial of Miliss to be conducted.'

Rocquel, who was still striving for recovery from his fateful error in having this discussion with her at all, said in his matter-of-fact voice, 'What I'm curious about is the nature of the charges he intends to level against her – '

Those charges surprised Dav more than Rocquel, who still nursed memories of his year away. He had learned something about humans during his absence, and could even control a certain Symbol himself – without, he realized, really understanding it.

Miliss was accused of being an enemy alien, illegally resident on Jana; spying for an invading alien force from space; conspiring to pretend to be a member of a decadent race when in fact she was a member of a superior, dominant race set down among primitives.

She was also charged with harbouring criminal intent.

Dav scanned the headlines unbelievingly, standing in the rain in front of a news-stand. Janae in colourful raincoats drifted past him as – directed by a guide sentence on page one – he turned to the editorial page. There he read in the language of Low Jana:

In an unprecedented action, the government today challenged the right to live on this planet of the two relics of an older civilization. Almost melodramatic charges of conspiracy were levelled at the couple, but only the woman has been arrested.

We propose to leave to the courts the resolution of the legal tangle implicit in this arrest, but find ourselves thoughtful about the matter on a strictly theoretical basis.

Explorers have recently found isolated tribes of Janae still living in stone-age cultures. Contact with our superior civilization was enacted as a depressant on the aspirations and mores of the backward peoples, and they have seemed unable to recover as a group.

Until today's governmental action, we have known a reverse condition with the two human beings resident on Jana. They represent an older culture – one that apparently had virtually died out for reasons never analysed. Such a decadent culture, even though it had clearly attained heights of scientific achievement far in advance of what is available on Jana, has not acted as depressant on spirit of the Janae.

Matters to be adjudicated by the courts include the following. Are Dav and Miliss representatives of a superior culture that is merely pretending to be decadent, so that the normal depressant impact upon an inferior culture is avoided? If so, does their presence here come under the heading of an alien conspiracy? And can such a purpose be interpreted as an invasion?

The account was perceptive. It indicated the presence of a highly intelligent professional class already in existence in Nunbrid and hundreds of other cities. The lower-class Janae had clearly matured more rapidly than their hereditary rulers. Yet the tone of the editorial was neither inflammatory nor antagonistic. In fact, it showed respect for the government and awareness of the meaning of the new law.

Dav's own thought ceased at that point. He had been aware that passersby were glancing at him. Now, suddenly, one big male stopped, uttered an explosive oath, and lifted an arm threateningly, as if to strike.

Dav shrank back involuntarily. The male grew instantly contemptuous and kicked at him. Dav, alert now, dodged with easy skill but dropped his newspaper. The big fellow scooped it up from the wet sidewalk and pounded the soggy sheets.

He roared, 'You've got to be nothing. You're the last of a vanished race. A nothing! A nothing!'

Dav retreated. He found a side street, slipped into its darker, damp distances, heading for home. As he approached the edge of the city, he heard a sound in the night ahead of him, a swelling murmur of ugly voices. Then, out in the open spaces between himself and his house, he saw a huge crowd carrying torches.

Startled, Dav withdrew from the open area and headed

for a small house on a nearby street. The place was actually a secret entrance to the big white mansion. Long ago, when Jana had been more primitive, unpleasant incidents had occurred. The secret access had often proved useful.

He made his way safely through the connecting tunnel to the big house, and from its interior gazed out at the crowd through a viewplate. The plate magically dissolved the night and the rain, showing a dull day-view of the large grounds in front of the house.

At first look the mob seemed even huger than he had estimated. Dav shook his head sadly. The pattern was the same as it had once been on old Earth. At the top was the hereditary hierarchy. Next came a law-abiding middle class of people. At the bottom seethed the vast mass of the unthinking.

The hierarchy was semi-psychotic, murderous, subjective. And the middle class was still relatively new and unaware of its future power. The mob was completely duped.

Dav observed with relief that several hundred troops patrolled an area between him and the angry crowd. An officer spoke through a loudspeaker system, addressing the mob.

'Go home. The rule of law shall prevail. Go home. If these people are spies, they will be judged by the law. Go home – '

The frequently repeated admonition began to have its effects towards midnight. Dav saw that there were fewer people outside, and more were drifting back towards the city. But it was nearly two in the morning before, feeling that the danger was over, he went to bed.

Lying there, he rejected the accusations against Miliss and himself with little more than a moment's consideration.

It was true, as the newspaper editorial had pointed out, that primitives had in the past suffered psychic and racial disaster as a result of being exposed abruptly to a superior culture. And, conceivably, somebody might mercifully evolve a more systematic approach to the problem.

But the mentors would know. That had to be. It would be absolutely ridiculous if Miliss and he weren't aware of their own realities.

All these hundreds of years of ignorance on so vital a point?

The truth was that simple and obvious. Nearly four hundred empty years made a weight of time in his mind that no words and no Jana accusation could penetrate.

He had no trouble sleeping.

Chapter V

Rocquel had stayed in the palace communications centre during the period of threat against Dav. Several times he spoke directly to the commanding officer of the troops patrolling the grounds.

At last, weary and a little guilty at having been out late again, he went to his apartment. The bedroom was dark as he entered and he had an instant, awful intuition.

He flicked on the light and stood confused and shaken. Nerda was in bed, undressed under the sheets. Her eyes were closed. Her breathing came with the regularity of sleep.

Rocquel's thought flashed back to their conversation of the morning and to his sudden feeling that he had ruined himself with her. His inability to grasp the meaning of the Symbol idea troubled him again.

Standing beside his sleeping wife, he visualized the repercussions of her rebellion if it were ever found out. His absence had shaken the throne, and he had returned too recently to have fully recovered his power and position. He had divined an uneasiness in the nobility – it would take a little while before those suspicious, violent beings were reassured that the new law was not a direct threat.

And if they found out that he was so weak that he could not control his wife – Instantly an old impulse propelled him towards her sleeping body. His hands and jaws clenched with the automatic effort that would shove her in a single thrust out of the far side of the bed.

He poised before that act, suddenly gripped and held by a thought and feeling new to him.

He had been about to act on the Jana-male attitude. But was Nerda justified in her rebellion? Was the old way the way women should be treated? Had his analysis of her reason for what she had done been accurate?

A flash of an old male paranoia darkened his face and mind – the absolute conviction that Nerda was doing this because another male had gotten to her.

Dav, the human?

Some portion of Rocquel's mind recognized the total irrationality of the thought – recognized that if it were true, Jana females would not associate with males of their own free will, they obviously did not betray their husbands. He was also aware that Dav, who had an unlimited sense of personal responsibility, would not have taken advantage of the queen's year of 'widowhood.'

The recognition and awareness were not enough for his fevered brain, alive with brutal images.

He had to know.

He turned and walked out of the room. Within minutes, he was part of a motorcycle army unit roaring through the night streets of Nunbrid towards the military prison where Miliss was confined.

The long, bleak concrete corridors of the prison echoed to his footsteps and those of his guards. The light carried by the prison's officer-of-the-night was bright enough, but it cast wavering shadows.

In that uneven brightness, Rocquel noted the grey drabness of this prison world, and some of the singleness of his purpose softened. The thought came to him that Miliss had been held here now for several days and that this was wrong.

He could do nothing about it under the new law, but within himself he felt a deep anger against Jaer.

The rage was brief. It ended as they reached Miliss's cell – and there she was. Rocquel went in alone, his guards retreating, waiting.

Their first moments together were ordinary. Miliss's surprise and pleasure when she recognized him, then her puzzlement that he should come at so late an hour, gave him his opening.

He asked her the question: Why had she and Dav separated?

The woman was startled. She sensed the dark purpose in him – who had always been so friendly to her and with whom she had communicated so well in the past.

After a moment, realizing that delay was unwise, she gave him Dav's diagnosis – that she had gone into the death thing that had destroyed man. She deemed it the best reply, considering all possibilities.

Her answer and its deadly implications for her shocked him out of his madness. She explained in greater detail.

Rocquel said, 'Then what you are saying is that you acted out of some parallel to the type of emotion used by people who actually did have the death thing. You did this consciously, knowing Dav would believe it was in fact the death thing.'

'I think that's what I did,' Miliss replied. She added quickly, 'The death thing is subtle. One can fool oneself.'

Rocquel persisted, 'But as far as you're concerned, you're not really dying?'

'As far as I know, I'm not.'

Rocquel considered that in a gathering amazement. Finally: 'But why aren't you doing something about getting out of this prison? You shouldn't be here.'

'What can I do?'

'Don't you have any protection of your own?'

'Nothing,' she said, 'but the Symbols so far activated. Except for a few hand weapons and mobile energy units, most of which we've given to the Janae, that's all we have.'

'What about other – later – Symbols?'

'Their time is not yet,' said Miliss. 'They wouldn't work – not for Jana.'

Rocquel sighed.

But, he wanted to say, Dav used the power of millions of believers in a constitutional monarchy before they ever believed in it – in fact, before they even knew about it. Why not use the power of millions of believers in some future Symbol before they ever believe in it?

He did not ask the question. The concept of any Symbol was beyond his ability to grasp. He realized humbly that he was a Jana nobleman of a somewhat simple nature and that the year he had spent aboard the earth battleship – the time he had described to no one – had been really like some tribal king's being . . . entertained, if that was the right word, by traders or scientists from a superior civilization. Being kindly disposed, they had been anxious not to hurt his feelings – but to them he had been a nothing. His status had been meaningless except insofar as they had a policy of using native kings in their interplanetary welfare work.

Nonetheless, he tried again to reach understanding.

At his request Miliss explained the power of a Symbol once more. But it didn't penetrate.

We thick-skulled males . . .

'And the ridiculous thing,' he explained his failure to Miliss, 'is that I myself actually have control of a Symbol –'

He stopped. It was an admission that he would have made to no other living person – only to this one individual with whom he had always felt able to speak freely.

He finished lamely, 'Of course, that was given to me as a protection.'

He stopped again because of the look on her face – intent, avid, seeking, startled, unbelieving but finally believing.

Miliss whispered, 'Who gave you control of that Symbol?'

'Human beings,' Rocquel said simply.

She sank back. She seemed to cringe on the cot, as if, like a mental patient, she were wracked by a psychic disease that contracted her body, curling it, twisting her head to one side.

Finally she said, 'Then Jaer's intuitions, accusations, may be true. There are human beings out there –' She suddenly broke off, breathless. 'Tell me exactly where you were, what you saw –'

Rocquel described his year on the battleship.

She whispered, 'There were both men and women?'

'Yes. It was a community of several thousand, I would say.'

'They never landed anywhere?'

'Not that I was aware of.' He sighed. 'But it was such a big ship. I saw only what appeared on the visual screens in the sections where I was permitted to wander. They didn't teach me the language. I only heard what the interpreting machines said to me.' He considered possibilities. 'Landing parties could have gone down to planets without my knowing it.'

'It was one of these humans that taught you control of a Symbol?'

'Yes.'

Miliss persisted. 'But what was it supposed to do? If Jaer had actually slashed at you with his sword – what would have happened to him?'

Rocquel didn't know.

He explained slowly, 'They warned me to be careful with

it – because if I wasn't, it would hook on to me, too.' He added: 'When I set it up against Jaer, I could feel it tugging at me, sort of like –' he paused, groping – 'maybe like a magnet.'

'But what is it a Symbol of?' Miliss asked.

Rocquel had no idea.

She went on, baffled: 'It must be drawing its energy from some meaningful idea on another planet – since we didn't sense anything here. But what could it be? No answer came to her, and she asked, 'You still have control of it?'

He nodded.

'Did they say they would let you maintain it permanently?'

Rocquel gazed at her unhappily. 'I can't remember. I was told something – but each time I think I'm going to recall it, it fades.'

'That sounds like close-to-the-surface programming,' Miliss nodded. 'As if whatever it relates to might happen at any time. So we must be near a crisis.' She added, obviously thinking out loud, that only a Symbol could act with subtle or powerful influence over distances. She finished: 'It must be very personal to you, which in itself is unusual. For example, if I could do what you have described – I could get out of this prison.'

Miliss's second admission of helplessness focused Rocquel's attention on her situation. Her confession that she could not protect herself was abruptly enormously significant. It placed control back in Jana hands. Janae could accept or reject a gift of knowledge from the reservoir on a self-determined basis.

We can use what they have, but we don't have to . . .

Rocquel felt somehow stronger in his Jana identity as he had that awareness. The accusations levelled at Miliss by Jaer had had a certain truth to them. The entire populace felt a displacement as a consequence of the human presence, gentle as it was.

After a little he was able to reason out the extent of her predicament. He was appalled. Her position was very severe if she and Dav could not really protect themselves.

With an effort he pushed aside his anxiety for her, grew calm and grave.

'There will be a difficult time ahead, my dear,' he said gently. 'The new law binds me as much as it does everyone else. I cannot arbitrarily set you free. Have you an attorney?'

'Not yet,' Miliss answered.

'I'll call Dav and tell him that it is imperative he get one for you.'

'He won't do a thing.' She reminded him of the death-drive situation – how only those survived who refused to help. She finished, 'I counted on that to keep him away from me. So there can be no help from him.'

Rocquel shook his head, smiling, and pointed out that his position in the matter was stronger than Dav's.

'I'll call him,' he said firmly. 'He'll do it because I ask him, not necessarily to help you.' He broke off. 'He's the one who should act in this matter. It will look odd if he doesn't. So he will.'

At that moment Rocquel accidentally caught a glimpse of his watch. It registered nearly four in the morning. He was instantly contrite.

'I'm sorry,' he apologized. 'I've kept you awake.'

Miliss brushed his words aside.

'I feel so much better. You've given me the first inform-ation from – out there –' she gazed upward, waved vaguely – 'that I've had in all the years Dav and I have been here. It's not clear – it's hard to decide what it means. But now I know that there are still a few other human beings.'

On that note they separated. Rocquel returned to the palace and presently slipped into bed beside the sleeping Nerda.

She was a problem to which he had no quick solution either.

Chapter VI

The Jana attorney whom Dav consulted shook his head gravely over the fourth count.

'The other accusations,' he said, 'have as yet no legal penalties. The judge could do anything, could even release her. But criminal intent has proved dangerous in the past. It can bring a capital verdict.'

Dav attended the trial as a witness, getting angrier every minute as all his 'gifts' to the Janae were used as evidence against Miliss. The argument of the State was that a

superior culture was, by way of its scientific gifts, cunningly
guiding the Janae away from their natural development and
into a mental enslavement that was the equivalent of a
takeover of one people by another. Dav's concern was with
the accusations, not with Miliss.

Called to the stand by Miliss's attorney, he denied all such
intent.

'Science is neutral,' he said. 'It is the truth of nature. Jana
scientists would normally and in due course have discovered
exactly the same truths. In giving the Janae the scientific
artifacts of Earth's ancient civilization, I fulfilled a duty
imposed upon me by a vanished race to hand on the torch of
knowledge as rapidly as feasible in the hope that, with such
a head start, the Janae would succeed in establishing a
permanent growing civilization instead of one that would
eventually dwindle as others, including men's, have been
them – '

When he later came out on the street a troop of guards
sent by Rocquel saved him from a demonstrating crowd.

KEEP YOUR FOREIGN SCIENCE . . . JANA MUST
BE FREED FROM THE ALIEN YOKE . . . JANA FOR
THE JANAE . . . DEATH TO THE INVADERS . . .
HUMANS, GO HOME –

The crowds screamed insults as Dav was escorted to a bus
that took him, accompanied by several guards, to the end of
the line. From there the soldiers walked with him to his
house, where other soldiers patrolled the approaches, back,
front, and sides.

Miliss was found guilty on all counts and sentenced to
death. Three appeals to ever higher courts failed. But
Rocquel granted her a full pardon on the grounds that the
Chosen had not legislated on the matters at issue.

'Prime Minister' Jaer Dorrish – and where had the title
come from? – thereupon introduced amendments to
criminal law. They were duly passed by the Chosen. Rocquel,
to Jaer's surprise, did not veto the legislation.

He asked Rocquel about it. The hereditary ruler gestured.

'I told you I wouldn't interfere.' He paused, curious.
'Suppose all those charges you're making turn out to be true.
If man is really a superior race, then presumably a fleet of
total power will come to the rescue of his representatives on
Jana – and we will all be degraded by having to submit,

however briefly, to an occupation force. What would you gain if that were to happen?'

Jaer scowled.

'Jana honour,' he said with the traditional arrogance of the Jana male, 'demands that the truth of this matter be brought out into the open. We shall deal with this so-called total power when we see it.'

'With what weapons?' Rocquel asked derisively.

Jaer said, 'The human man is being watched night and day. At the proper moment we'll make a raid and we'll capture all man's scientific secrets and make an end of this degrading dole system on which he seems to have been operating – one secret at a time. Such doling is an unbearable insult. We want to have everything – now!'

Rocquel stared sardonically at the other's flushed face.

Finally he said sceptically, 'Your concern with such minor matters does not fit with your previous character, Jaer. I wonder what you're really up to.'

The big male stiffened. 'Do you question my loyalty, sire?'

It could have been a dangerous moment. But Rocquel merely shook his head chidingly.

'No, Jaer. I expect you will accept the new law. It is to your advantage. What is your next move?'

'You'll see.'

Jaer turned abruptly and walked away.

Later Rocquel sought out Nerda, reported Jaer's statements, and asked her opinion.

She answered at once – no longer a surprise to him. Ever since her rebellion on the matter of going to sleep without his permission – which she now did as a matter of course – she had been freer in her responses in every way, even in their personal relations.

She told him that in her opinion Jaer wanted the human woman and that therefore his real target in the trial was not Miliss but Dav.

Rocquel stared at his wife.

'But – ' he began, and stopped.

Careful, he thought. Don't give her another reason for losing respect for you. No knowing what repercussions that would have . . .

But he felt slightly helpless before her statement. What she suggested was an immensely tricky thing for Jaer to be doing. Presumably the head of the Dorrish clan expected that Miliss would be freed.

Rocquel's thought paused, a light dawning. Of course, in the trial of Miliss all the weaknesses of the prosecution's case – and the strength of the defence – would be revealed, whereupon all the various loopholes in the law would be rectified – at which time Dav would be tried and irrevocably convicted.

Rocquel stepped forward impulsively, and embraced Nerda.

'You're very brilliant,' he said. 'There's no question – I've got a very unusual and perceptive queen. Thank you.'

He kissed her and was aware for the barest instant that she kissed him back. The action must have been involuntary. She broke the kiss and became passive.

Rocquel was not offended. In the back of his mind was the thought that Jana females were, perhaps, not as un-emotional as was believed.

It might be worthwhile some day to conduct a deeper experiment.

Meanwhile – he had to warn Dav.

The next morning Rocquel learned that Miliss, who had been returned to custody on the formal charge of being a danger to the realm, was to be retried. Her attorney's plea at the preliminary hearing that afternoon was double jeopardy and the inapplicability of retroactive legislation.

The judge released her.

The prosecution requested and got a warrant for the arrest of Dav.

The evening paper reported that the arresting officers had failed to find the Earth man.

Dav spent the late afternoon in one of the hiding places of the Reservoir of Symbols, planning his escape.

It was time for the kind of disappearance that Miliss and he in times past had occasioanlly had to undertake. There had been other Janae like Jaer Dorrish. They, too, had had their own remorseless purposes. Escape in those distant times had almost always consisted of their waiting somewhere for the particualr enemy to live out his short life span.

Dav left his hiding place after dark and made his way

through the brush. His desination was a certain hillside where, nearly seventy years ago, he had buried a small spaceship.

In years gone by, such long-buried machinery had not always been readily located when needed – but this one had survived its seven decades totally free of unpleasant accidents. No bulldozer had nosed near it. No one had perched a building on top of it. The craft waited for him in its temporary grave.

Dav was carefully clearing away a particularly dense clump of tall shrubs when he heard a sound. Noiselessly he sank to the ground.

Too late. He heard a swift pad of footsteps in the dark. Two pairs of eyes glowed at him from beside some brush. Then strong, lean fingers had him pinned down.

The unmistakable long nose of a Jana male was silhouetted against the haze of city lights. A Jana female stood beyond him.

The deep voice of the male said exultantly, 'Got you. Perna, quick, come over here and turn a light on this spying rascal – ' The words halted on a curse. 'By Dilit, it isn't that scoundrel suitor of yours after all. Perna, bring that light, and let's see what we've got here.'

There was silence except for the unhurrying footsteps of the female.

Dav lay unresisting. He could have taken steps. He could have reached up and, with the enormous strength that he could focus into any part of his body, with unerring fingers stabbed at the two vital nerve centres in the Jana, to send the big male sprawling in agony. Or he could simply have contemptuously and effortlessly disengaged himself by a direct muscular thrust.

He did neither. As in past times, he was prepared to act defensively according to the need.

A blaze of light cut off his thought. The light beat pitilessly down on his upturned face. And then, the female's voice came, thick with disgust.

'Why, it's the man. So this is the kind of lover you protect me from. Bah!'

'Not so fast with your critisicm,' growled the male. 'There's a reward. We can get married.' His grip tightened on Dav. 'Get up, you antique. It's time you and that woman ceased hanging on to life. Your kind is dead.'

The moment for action had arrived, but Dav did nothing. He offered no resistance as he was jerked roughly to his feet.

In those moments, an astounding thing had happened.

He did not care.

His thought was: *Man's civilization is dead – why should Miliss and I be bound by the values of a society that has failed?*

The barriers he had erected against Miliss collapsed, and a great guilt overwhelmed him. Suddenly he saw how rigid he had been as the dedicated saviour of a new race.

In that prolonged moment of anguish, something she had once said flashed in his memory.

I'm sure even your nose is getting a little longer. Pretty soon you'll even look like the Janae –

He had lived in a dream, he saw now, a kind of self-induced hypnotism – an ideal which had given a temporary significance to an otherwise meaningless existence.

With Miliss doomed, nothing here was worth saving.

He went wordlessly with his captor.

The news came to Rocquel in the small hours of the morning that Dav had been arrested. He left his bed, dressed, phoned Miliss.

'Have you had a visitor yet?'

'No. But I imagine he'll be here soon.'

Rocquel said, 'I'm coming right over.'

He arrived by way of the secret entrance, and walked along a narrow, dim-lit corridor until he came to a closed door.

Voices sounded from beyond it.

Rocquel drew the door towards him and stepped through. He found himself in an alcove lighted by reflections from a bright room beyond a green and gold screen. The voices came from the other side of the screen. He recognized the calm bass of Jaer Dorrish and Miliss's indignant soprano.

'I'm surprised,' Miliss was saying, 'that you continue to pursue me despite the fact that you are probably personally programmed and may be in grave danger.'

Jaer answered her with complete assurance, 'I once allowed myself to be alarmed by such words. That will not happen again.'

'What you're saying,' said Miliss sharply, 'is that you've abandoned reason.'

'The Jana male,' was the cool reply, 'knows what is important. A female is. Motivations for fear are not.' He chuckled lazily. 'Let me reason out this situation for you. If you resist me, you may be arrested again. But I may not even press charges against Dav if you give in. Who knows what privileges may continue for you two if you and I occasionally meet privately during the many, otherwise dull years ahead.'

Rocquel stood there behind the screen and shook his head. Nerda's intuition was correct. This entire action against the human beings was simply a typical Jana-male scheme in connection with a female.

He was not shocked. Or surprised, really.

Jaer said, 'It is late, my dear. Surely you do not expect any other visitors this evening.'

The remark made it the ideal moment for Rocquel to come out of his hiding place.

'What I said to him,' he told Nerda after he returned to the palace, 'was, "Jaer, if I'm going to surrender some of the prerogatives of the crown – it is because I believe you and others of the nobility, in exchange for greater political power, will give up the purely personal privileges of forcing individuals to yield to a lordly whim." '

'And what did he answer?'

'Nothing. He turned and walked out of the room and out of the house.'

Nerda made a distasteful gesture.

'If he can get rid of Dav, he'll count on eventually forcing Miliss to accept his protection.'

'Then you think he will press charges against Dav?'

'Your words didn't reach him. He's still an old-style Jana male.' She shrugged. 'So, of course.'

Dav sat apathetic throughout his trial. The defence attorney appointed by Rocquel could not even persuade him to testify on his own behalf.

He was convicted of being an alien spy and sentenced to be beheaded.

Chapter VII

By the time Rocquel's helicopter settled down on the big compound where the executions would take place, the male nobility was milling around inside, catcalling and gambling. The wagers usually consisted of someone's maintaining that he would win the chance to chop off the head of a convicted person.

Rocquel walked through the crowd of would-be executioners, hearing grumbling about the increasing shortage of criminal heads. He came to the roped-off area where the victims were guarded and saw what the problem was. Fewer than a hundred males, including Dav – and four females – were herded together at one end of an area that in the past had often held as many as five hundred.

Roughly one hundred heads were to be divided among nearly eighteen hundred eager young nobles.

Rocquel was handed the list of the doomed. Silently he scanned down it, looking for identifying comments. His attention caught two names. Their owners were classified as engineers. He scowled and turned to Jaer.

'What are valuable men like that doing on this list?'

Jaer held up a hand in a demanding way.

'Your Majesty,' he said in a formal tone. 'I must call to your attention that you are violating the procedure of the new law. The king can no longer deal directly with individual cases. As your prime minister, I will consult you or listen to your advice and, in some instances but not all, will recommend that you grant mercy. Please give me that list.'

With a sinking sensation Rocquel handed it over. He had been intent on trying to save Dav and had automatically, as in times past, taken charge. He grew aware that the big male Jana was smiling satirically.

'As for your question, sire,' Jaer said blandly, 'the new law specifies that all prisoners are subject to due process and to similar penalties.' He shrugged. 'They killed. They were tried. The sentence was automatic.'

'I see,' said Rcoquel.

What he saw most of all was that the noisy crowd would be against Dav and that he had no solution to his problem of how to save the human.

Jaer was speaking again.

'Would you like to have me single these males out for questioning, sire?'

The Jana prime minister's tone was tantalizing. He clearly felt himself in total ascendancy in this situation and was prepared to play hard at the game of constitutional monarchy. It seemed so obviously in his favour.

Rocquel nodded yes to the question. While the two doomed males were being located, he consciously forced himself to remember his old way of dealing with one thing at a time. Presently he was able to put the fate of the human being out of the forefront of his mind and concentrate his attention on the here and now.

The scene that he was thus able to focus on was almost literally right out of old Jana. He saw everywhere the swishing silks of the nobles, a glinting ocean of changing colours. Each male's head was an elongated red shape that was visible at about the same height above the almost solid wall of silk. Eighteen hundred such heads made a picture of – oddly enough – innocent beauty.

But it was the beauty of a beast of prey, proud, arrogant, strong, untamed. It was as if a natural state of being were on display. The primitive impulses that still moved these males from violence to violence in a never-ending madness were the product of equally primitive necessities – their truth unquestioned on Jana until Dav and Miliss had begun to force self-control on a hierarchy that lived by the bloody law of supermasculinity.

I am looking, thought Rocquel, on the end of an era. Here, in these eighteen hundred, is embodied the last of the really feudal thing . . .

It had to go, of course. But how?

His thought ended as the two scientists were brought before Jaer. The Dorrish male glanced questioningly at Rocquel, who stepped forward. A moment later he was confronting their reality.

Professional scientists and all technical personnel had received special treatment from the courts for many years. They were not let off totally free, as a noble might be, but were given a preferred status. A person with an advanced degree was proclaimed to be the equal of twenty ordinary persons. Possession of a secondary degree made him the equivalent of fifteen persons. And the lowest degree, ten. Technicians started at two and went up to nine.

Thus a twenty-person engineer who killed a wholly non-professional individual suffered what was only a one-twentieth penalty – usually a fine. Only if he killed another scientist of a twenty-person status was he in serious danger of being executed. That was murder by law.

Jaer was speaking.

'Here they are, sire. I don't really see that we can do anything for them under the new regulations.'

Rocquel had the same thought. But he said nothing as Jaer turned away and ordered the males to be brought closer. The two engineers came forward and were identified as, respectively, a fifteen and a ten. The former had killed in a fit of rage, which – when his gag was removed – he earnestly protested had been a proper reaction to an insolent three. And the ten had killed a unit person in a fit of typical Jana-male temper for no particular reason.

No occasion existed for favouritism. The new law must convince by its impartiality. The two were simply unlucky that they were the first examples of their class.

Rocquel nodded. Jaer had the gags replaced and then read in a loud, clear voice the confirmation of the sentences.

Moments later the lottery machine drew the names of the executioners. And, to the sound of much cursing on the part of those who had lost, the grinning winners came forward, simultaneously raised their swords, and simultaneously struck at the heads on the blocks.

And missed.

A roar of amazement came from the gallery of noble Janae.

Rocquel was fighting a peculiar confusion. Something – some energy – had snatched at one side of his body, pulled at one arm, spun him slightly. At that moment the yelling started, and he realized that something was wrong.

He whirled.

The two nobles had recovered. Muttering words of outrage, they raised their swords for a second blow.

'Wait!' Rocquel roared.

The swords wavered, were sullenly grounded. Two angry, embarrassed nobles glared at their hereditary king questioningly.

'What happened?' Rocquel demanded.

Both told the same story.

Something like a wind had snatched at their swords. Or it was as if they had struck at a blast of air so strong it had diverted their slashing blows.

Catcalls were beginning among the onlookers. Rocquel glanced unhappily at the prison compound and saw that Dav had come to the gate.

Rocquel spoke to Jaer.

'Let nothing happen till I return.'

The Dorrish leader gave him a startled look but said nothing as Rocquel walked over to where Dav stood.

The human greeted him with: 'What happened?'

'That's what I was going to ask you.'

He explained what the nobles had said.

'Sounds like a Symbol,' Dav admitted, frowning. 'But I know of none that is applicable in a situation such as this. Due process has occurred. There's nothing better on Jana right now. Why don't you have Jaer continue with the executions? Maybe it was an accident.'

Rocquel, who was remembering the grabbing sensation that had affected his right side moments before, and also on the morning of his return to Jana, silently doubted it. But he walked back to the executioners' blocks and ordered the two engineers released. That was the tradition.

'You forfeit your wagers,' he curtly told the would-be executioners.

The two males walked off, cursing.

The order of procedure now required that the females be killed. One of the four was a poor little old thing who was quite insane. She believed the crowd was present to fete her. It did not even occur to Rocquel to do anything for her. Jana had no place for insane people. They were invariably put to death if they became a burden – and a burden she was.

As Rocquel turned to consider the other females, he found his way barred by Jaer. The big male was shaking his head.

'Sire,' he said, 'you have been taking command again.'

The truth was obvious. Rocquel shook his head.

74

He said with a twisted smile, 'Giving up power seems to be quite a difficult process. So bear with me, Lord Jaer. I mean well.'

No answering smile moved that grim countenance.

Rocquel thought, *What a remarkable man the ancient king on earth must have been who first agreed – when there were no precedents – to limit his absolute rights under a constitutional monarchy . . .*

At the moment he could not remember the name of that king, though Dav had told him.

What brought the historic precedent to mind was that, even now, Rocquel found it hard to adjust to the idea that what he gave up, Jaer would gain. But finally Rocquel relaxed.

He stepped back.

'Continue, Lord of the Dorrish.'

He was able then to observe the scene once more without interference from his troubled inner self.

Of the other three females, two were beyond anyone's power to help. They had been accused of adultery by their noble husbands and had been convicted. Rocquel privately doubted that the unnatural crime had occurred, but this was not the time to take issue with a court's findings.

The remaining woman had denied the truth of religion. As she was brought before them, Jaer glanced questioningly at Rocquel. He evidently expected no interference, intended the glance to be a matter of form only.

He was turning away when Rocquel caught his arm.

The Dorrish leader faced about with a tolerant expression. It became quite evident, as he listened to Rocquel, that on these minor matters he was prepared to allow the king the prerogative of granting mercy.

He finally said, 'Sire, why don't I say that in this instance a reprieve will be granted and then you state the reasons.'

That was the way it was done.

Rocquel spoke briefly to the assembled nobles, stressing the need – as Dav had urged upon him long ago – to keep religion humanitarian.

He spared her life.

He stood by then, tense, not knowing what to expect as the three overjoyed winners came forward. The two who were assigned the adulterous females uttered expressions of pleasure at having the privilege of performing so necessary a task.

All three swords whipped high and came down as one.

The females had been kneeling fatalistically. They looked up after a little as if to ask what was wrong.

What was wrong was that the swords were lying a dozen feet away – Rocquel, who had watched closely, thought he had seen the glint of too much metal as the weapons had flown through the air. But he could not be sure. Something strong had grabbed at him, as with fingers of steel, and had moved him inches at the moment of attempted execution.

He saw that Jaer was lying on the ground nearby. Rocquel helped the big male to his feet.

'What happened?'

'This is magic,' Jaer muttered. 'Something hit me a terrific blow.'

He seemed uncertain and offered no objection to Rocquel's suggestion that the executions should be temporarily halted, pending an investigation.

'But what kind of investigation?' he asked in a bewildered tone.

Rocquel assured him that there was at least one person to question.

And so, after the women had been released and the second group of executioners dismissed, Rocquel had Dav brought out of the compound.

'You saw that?' he asked accusingly.

'Yes. There's no doubt. It's a Symbol, and the second time it was more violent. The power behind it is increasing very rapidly.'

'But what Symbol can it be?' Rocquel protested. 'I thought Symbols were – ' He stopped, remembering that he had no idea what Symbols were. He finished lamely: 'What do you suggest?'

Dav said, 'The next time there may be feedbacks, and the executioners may get hurt.' He seemed interested. Some of the apathy he had displayed earlier seemed to be lifting. His eyes were suddenly bright. He looked around hopefully. 'Why don't you let Jaer try to execute me? That would solve a lot of problems.'

Rocquel frowned. He shook his head. Injury to – or the death of – the head of the Dorrish clan would merely create confusion in an important segment of the Jana populace.

The catcalls were beginning again, demanding decisions. But the nobles sounded puzzled. The tone of the raised voices showed that the vocalizers were not clear as to what was going on. And only a percentage was actually yelling. It struck Rocquel that to the aristocratic onlookers the events at the focal point of the executions had probably been obscure.

Besides, no one had ever been able to explain anything, really, to Jana nobles as a group.

The fact that no help could be expected from the nobility made the situation even more difficult. Rocquel stood distracted, not knowing what to do. The yelling grew louder, more insistent. Abruptly Rocquel realized why. By bringing Dav out of the compound he had given the impression that the human was next in line for exectuion.

And Dav's life was what those who cried out were demanding.

Dav was pale but yelled above the bedlam almost directly into Rocquel's ear. 'Why not make the attempt? Let's see what happens.'

Rocquel tried to answer back, tried to say, *What's going on? What's happening? Is the Symbol I believed I had control of acting independently of my command – or any command at all?*

He couldn't say it. The words wouldn't come. His face contorted with his effort to speak.

Dav asked, 'What's the matter, sire?'

Rocquel tried again to speak, could not. A degrading awareness overwhelmed him.

I'm programmed. I could tell Miliss about the Symbol I controlled, but I can't tell Dav . . .

Not – the realization suddenly was strong – that he had ever really controlled it. It had been attached to him some-how – but in the manner of a Symbol it had reacted in this situation because this was what it related to.

'I feel,' said Rocquel – and now the words came easily – 'that these executions are not being allowed.'

So he could speak if he made no direct reference to his Symbol.

Dav was shaking his head.

'I don't understand it. The time is not yet on Jana for the

77

end of capital punishment. In fact – ' He sounded appalled. He waved vaguely, his gesture taking in the horizon. 'If a few million of those paranoid males out there ever get the idea that they cannot be executed, all hell will break loose.'

The picture of total disaster – of pillage, rape, and mayhem – evoked by the man's words sent a chill through Rocquel. He visualized vast armies of criminals rioting in the streets, swarming in gangs through the country. Something had to be done at once.

Belatedly, again he remembered that the Dorrish leader was in charge here and should be consulted. He swung about and became aware that the big male was standing off to one side, watching Dav from narrowed eyes.

Rocquel had time for only a glance – the seconds were flying by, and the noise from the gallery was rising to such a crescendo that further conversation was impossible. Rocquel signalled the royal drummers to beat for silence.

Moments later he explained to a startled audience what Dav had said about a Symbol's being involved.

When he had finished, a loud voice cried from somewhere in the crowd, 'If we mob that so-and-so it'll end the nonsense.'

Whoever spoke must have tried to push forward. A movement started. A dozen, then dozens, then hundreds surged forward.

A voice yelled in Rocquel's ear, 'Run for your life – '

The tone was so urgent that Rocquel was a score of feet towards safety before he realized that it was Dav who had yelled at him. He stopped and turned – and was barely in time to see the disaster.

Chapter VIII

Male bodies were being spun as if in a whirlpool. A fountain was already up in the air, being held and twisted by an invisible force.

From the corner of one eye he saw Dav frantically pushing through the retreating crowd towards him. The human broke through abruptly.

'Quick!' he yelled. 'It they're whirled any higher, they may be hurt or killed when they fall.'

Rocquel said blankly, 'What do you mean – quick? Quick what?'

Dav's eyes, so bright for a moment, misted. A puzzled look came to his face.

He muttered, 'What's the matter with me? I don't know why I said that.'

But the real message of his reaction had penetrated. Rocquel was thinking. *He's programmed also . . .*

He felt the truth grow in him. It bothered him. Bothered him a lot. But the truth was that he was unquestionably watching the Symbol over which he had been given control.

What was reassuring was the fact that in this decisive hour the ultimate decision had been left to the hereditary general of Jana – himself.

As he hastily evoked within his mind the mental pattern that would bring the Tizane energy to bear on the Symbol, Rocquel thought, *It really doesn't take very much direct interference with individuals to control a planet with Symbols. Only a few key persons . . .*

In the entire sequence of events, the most unique facet was that both of the mentors – Dav and Miliss – had also not been allowed free will.

After the whirlpool of noble males of Jana began to drop to the ground – where some lay for a long time – Rocquel suggested to Jaer that the executions continue.

The big male stared at him blankly.

'Your Majesty,' he said finally in amazement. 'I doubt we could find a single person at this moment willing to act the role of executioner.'

Rocquel was convinced of it. He worded his reply blandly. The decision to suspend executions must be made by the government and not by the constitutional monarch.

He added, watching Jaer closely: 'I have a feeling that the government should also grant a pardon to Dav.'

Those words got him, first, a dark, darting look. Slowly a crooked smile stretched across that normally grim face.

'Your Majesty,' said Jaer Dorrish, 'let me refer to an earlier remark of yours. I have realized today that you do mean well and that it is hard to give up power. Apparently it is almost as hard for a person like myself to accept an accretion of power gracefully – but I should like to assure

79

you that it is my intention to try. I see the role of prime minister as one that will involve a great deal of integrity. So – ' He made a gesture with one hand, said in a formal tone, 'To prove to you that I have the intent of living up to that level of integrity, I hereby request in my capacity as leader of the government until the first election under the new law that you grant a reprieve and full pardon to Dav, the human.'

'I grant it,' said Rocquel.

It was a great victory – yet he experienced a sudden drop in spirits on the way home. He rode nearly a hundred yards with his motorcycle guard before he realized that he was having a more severe recurrence of an earlier feeling.

I'm programmed, and that degrades me . . .

Back in the palace, he told Nerda his feeling. All the rest of that afternoon and part of the evening, she argued with him.

Programming, she pointed out, was like a drop of chemical which might give to a flowing stream a slightly bluish tinge. Nothing but a dam could stop or divert the stream – yet after the injection of the chemical it was coloured in a specific way.

Her analogy triggered a thought in Rocquel. His programming had taken the form of accelerated civilizing of a paranoid male – himself. He was still hereditary general, still married to Nerda, with no intention of giving up either the position or the wife. Yet he had tolerated a change in the form by which he exercised his power, and he had accepted less total control over his wife.

And in neither instance did he feel a real loss.

Nerda suggested to him that the long-term programming of Miliss and Dav had been designed to make it possible for them to accept the unendurable existence of a lovely human couple marooned on an alien planet. And because the stream of life flowed immortally through them, they were separately programmed as a man and a woman to survive periodic crises. So the great civilization out there controlled even its own emissaries.

In this generation, Nerda continued, perhaps only she and Rocquel would know the truth and, to a lesser extent, Jaer. The hereditary general and his wife, and the hereditary leader of the principal subordinate group, the Dorrish. But their own personalities remained overwhelmingly private.

The stream of Jana identity flowed on in them – but it was now a more civilized being that felt the flow.

She must have realized from the accepting expression of his face and body that she could finally change the subject.

'Do you still have control of the Symbol?' she asked.

It was night, and they were standing at a huge window looking towards the slickrock mountains.

Rocquel imaged the first three stages of the Tizane pattern. Something grazed his leg. He knew a hackles-raising sensation – a sense of an energy field of enormous power.

Hastily he turned his thoughts aside.

'Yes,' he said. 'It's still there.'

'In your presence,' said Nerda, 'no one can be killed – as long as you control that Symbol. Did they say when they would take it away from you?'

Rocquel was about to make the same reply he had given to Miliss – when he realized that there was quite a different awareness in him. A barrier had lifted from his memory. He recalled exactly what he had been told.

'No,' he said simply, 'they just gave it to me. It's a lifetime gift.'

He began to feel better.

In my presence, no one can be killed . . .

Suddenly he divined that his was a very advanced Symbol indeed. He stood at a nearly unthinkable height of understanding and power.

Deep inside him something that was almost infinitely savage was mollified. Possessing what was surely one of the ultimate human Symbols – he accepted his lesser than human status.

For Dav it felt strange to be free. He walked slowly to a nearby restaurant and sat down at a table. He was eating almost mindlessly when he heard the radio announce that he had been pardoned. The news struck him with an odd impact. The life force within him quickened.

He grew aware that the Janae in the restuarant were staring at him curiously. No one showed hostility.

He had no place that he wanted to go – so later he walked the streets. Finally he began to wonder.

Am I trying to solve a problem – and if so, what?

He could not decide. Everything seemed very far away.

He had a feeling that there was something he should be doing. But he did not know what.

Night came.

He waved a surface car to a halt. It drew up, its lights glittering, its bells clanging. No one said anything to him as he swung aboard.

Some younger Janae climbed on at the next stop. They sat giggling at him. But they rushed off into a brilliantly lighted park where hundreds of youthful Janae were dancing to the rhythm of a low, fast-tempo, sobbing music.

He continued his public exposure until almost midnight, without any untoward incidents. He returned to the white house by the river. As he entered the west wing, he presumed Miliss was in her part of the residence. But he made no effort to contact her.

He slept the special deep sleep which triggered long-ago programming deep in his brain. Still asleep, he went to a room that was deceptively equipped with what seemed to be ordinary Jana-level electronic equipment. But by pressing certain buttons and turning certain dials in a specific sequence, Dav activated a communications system hidden in a remote part of the Jana planet.

Subspace radio waves thereupon transmitted a message to a receiver many light-years away.

The message was: 'The crisis of the last stage of kings has passed – '

The message completed automatically, then repeated and repeated. Finally a relay was closed on the receiving planet by an accepting mind.

A voice – or a thought – said, 'Message received, recorded.'

A light flashed on in an instrument in front of Dav and, still asleep, he returned to bed.

Miliss had watched him first through scanners and then – as she realized his catatonic unawareness of his surroundings – by following him closely.

So that, as he turned away from the equipment, she stepped up to it and spoke to the distant listener. It was almost as if her communication were expected.

The voice answered, 'We have come to a time when the woman – you – must know something of the truth.'

'What is the truth?' Miliss asked. She did not wait for the

reply, but rushed on: Was there a universal death, or was the idea the result of early programming?

'At the next crisis,' was the reply, 'you will be allowed to visit – and see for yourself. Meanwhile, the man – Dav – must not be told. In fact, you will discover if you try that you cannot tell him.'

'Why not tell him?'

It seemed that the reasons for that were deeply bound up in the godlike cravings of masculinity in the male and related idealistic motivations.

'And that's all we are allowed to say,' concluded the faraway voice.

When the connection had been broken, Miliss – feeling suddenly much better, even lighthearted, as if she were again somebody and not a living artifact of a dead culture; feeling strangely tender towards that poor, programmed superbeing, her husband – began the long task of moving back into the west wing.

By morning she had most of her beautiful things in their proper locations. And so, when Dav awakened and turned over, he saw a blonde woman with a smile on her face – and a faint look of innocence, as if everything she had done, including this return, had been totally rational.

This vision said to him, 'I hope you'll be glad to know that you have a wife again.'

On a planet where there is only one woman, and that woman beautiful, what could the only man say to that?

Dav said he was glad.

'Come over here,' he said.

THE PROBLEM PROFESSOR

Chapter I TEST RUN

Merritt recognized the crisis when VA-2 attained a speed of 4000 miles an hour.

Modelled on the German V-2 bomb, the rocket climbed towards the noonday sun on a column of crooked fire, as its gyroscopic stabilizers worked in their spasmodic fashion to balance the torpedo stucture.

Loaded with instruments instead of a warhead it shot up 764 miles. It topped the highest peak of the planet's 500-mile-deep atmosphere. It broke into the emptiness of space and, for a few moments on the television screen near the launching rack, the stars showed as bright pinpoints against a background of black velvet.

In spite of its velocity it was never in danger of leaving Earth's gravitational field. It came down. And, after they had exhumed the scarred shell from the desert sands, there was a meeting at which Merritt was appointed a committee of one. He was charged with the positive duty of persuading the government of the United States 'to finance and build a spaceship capable of transporting human beings in and through the airless void above the atmosphere of this planet.'

The sum of one thousand dollars was voted him for initial expenses.

* * * * *

Merritt tiptoed into his apartment about two o'clock. His excitement, now that he was home and near Ilsa, subsided rapidly. As he undressed in the living room, using only one dim light, he wondered what Isla would think of his mission.

'Bob, is that you?'

Merritt hesitated.

'What time is it, Bob?'

Merritt, carrying his shoes, trousers, coat and shirt, walked into the bedroom. Isla was sitting up, lighting a cigarette. She was a dark-haired olive-complexioned young woman with passionate lips. She put out her hand and Merritt handed her the cheque and, while she studied it, he climbed into his pyjamas and explained what it was for. She began to laugh before he finished, a staccato laugh.

'With one thousand dollars,' she said finally, controlling herself, 'you expect to persuade a *political* government to build a machine more expensive than any battleship ever constructed. My dear, I was married to a Washington lobbyist and I assure you it isn't done on the cheap.'

It was the first time in the four years since their marriage that she had mentioned her first husband. Merritt glanced at her sharply. He saw that her cheeks were flushed, that she was furious with him.

'Really,' she said, 'I wish you wouldn't waste your time with that bunch of dreamers. Spaceships! Such nonsense. Besides, what good is it? I wish you'd get busy and make some money for us.'

Merritt did not answer. He had a theory about money-making. But it was not one he could expound to a woman whose first husband had amassed a fortune after she divorced him.

He climbed into his bed. 'You have no object, I hope,' he said, 'to my spending the thousand before I come around to your way of thinking?'

Ilsa shrugged. 'It'll give you a trip. But it's so silly. What are you going to do first?'

'Go see a schoolmate of mine named Norman Lowery. He's secretary to Professor Hillier, the mathematician and physicist. We have to build up to the President by degrees, you know.'

'I'll bet you do,' said Ilsa.

She began to laugh again. She was still at it when Merritt made his first attempt to kiss her. She pushed him away.

'Don't try to get around me,' she said bitterly. 'I'm just beginning to realize that I'm doomed to be the wife of a low-salaried husband. You'll have to be gentle with me while I get used to the idea.'

Merrit said nothing. Life had become progressively tense

of recent months.

Almost, he had come to believe that men with obsessions shouldn't marry. It was too hard on the woman.

'The trouble with you,' said Ilsa, her voice softening, 'is that you're a living misrepresentation. You give the impression that you're bound for the top but you don't even try to get started.'

'Maybe I'm further along than you think,' Merritt ventured.

'*Nuts!*'

She finally let him kiss her – on the neck, not the lips. 'I feel as if I would poison you after what I've said. And I'm not quite prepared for that yet.'

* * * * *

Norman Lowery met Merritt at the station. He looked older by at least ten years than when Merritt had seen him two years previously. He led Merritt towards an imposing Cadillac and, after they had started, said, 'Don't be too surprised when you see Professor Hillier.'

That was Merritt's first inkling that something was wrong. 'What do you mean?' Sharply.

'You'll see.'

Merritt studied his friend's profile in narrow-eyed thoughtfulness but he asked no questions. The big car was out of the town now, bowling along a paved highway at sixty miles an hour.

After about ten minutes it turned off into a valley and came presently to a little dream village. Several large buildings dominated the scene. And there were about two dozen houses in all, scattered along the banks of a pretty winding stream.

As Lowery turned up the driveway of the largest bungalow he said, 'Professor Hillier is independently wealthy – luckily for him – and all this is his property. Those buildings over there are his labs. His assistants and their families live in the houses.'

He added, 'Notice how we're closed in by steep hills. That's in case of an atomic bomb attack on the big dam twenty-five miles south. All the buildings, including the residences, are steel and concrete under their stucco exteriors and panelled interiors, though the professor only laughs at that in his sensible moments.'

Merritt did not like the reference to 'sensible moments.' As the car parked in the driveway he climbed out slowly and took another look along the valley.

He thought, 'To me atomic energy is open sesame to the future. To these people – '

He wasn't sure just what was wrong. But there was a pressing negativeness here as if a man had built himself a mausoleum and was waiting for death to step closer. Long before, Merritt had rejected headlong retreat from the vulnerable cities, had aligned himself with the hundred million whose only hope of escape was that their leaders would have the common sense to solve the problem of the doomsday bomb.

Merrit asked finally, 'Has this place got a name?'

'Hillier Haven.'

At least it fitted.

They entered the house through french windows, which opened into a spacious living-room. There was a bar in one corner. Lowery ducked through an opening in its side and popped up behind it.

'I'll mix you a drink,' he said, 'then go look for the professor. This is his house, you know, or did I say that before? He and his daughter and I live here. Very cosy.' He laughed grimly. 'What'll you have?'

Merritt had a whisky and soda. He sat down in an easy chair and watched Lowery disappear into the garden beyond the french windows. The minutes passed. After about half an hour he climbed to his feet and walked over to a half-open door that had been intriguing him for some time. It was a library lined with books. Merritt returned to his chair. He was an avaricious reader but not today – not this month.

Another half-hour went by. He could feel himself growing tenser. He had already paced the length of the room several times. Now he did it again but without any sense of relaxation.

He had a vision of himself during the next few months, waiting for men like Professor Hillier to condescend to give him a hearing. He began to realize the massiveness of the task he had set himself. He was going to try to push an idea into men who had hacked their own way to success through the equivalent of granite.

Men whose characters were as different and inflexible as their achievements. Men of great talent and great power. He, Robert Merritt, who could scarcely pay his bills every month, was going to do all that.

'We're nuts!' he thought. 'The whole bunch of us. Imagine – a few hundred fanatics trying to push America into a spaceship! Ilsa was right.'

But he stayed where he was.

A door opened, and a girl came in. She was slim and blonde with grey eyes. She paused as she saw Merritt. She came forward, smiling.

'You must be Robert Merritt,' she said. 'Norman told me about you. I'm Drusilla Julia, Professor Hillier's daughter.'

She looked cool and refreshing and sane. Merritt answered her smile and said, 'Your father must be a student of ancient Rome.'

'Oh, you recognize the origin of my names.' She was pleased.

After a moment however she frowned. 'Norman has been telling me about what your club is trying to do. Just what are your plans?'

Merritt told her what VA-2 had accomplished. He went on, 'VB-Two is now under construction. It will be somewhat different from the first ship – ' he hesitated – 'in that its acceleration will never be above six gravities.'

He watched her face to see if she had any inkling of what that meant. For a moment she didn't seem to. And then her eyes lighted up.

She said in a low, intense tone, 'You're going to put a human being into it. You wonderful men! You wonderful young men! The future really does belong to you, doesn't it?'

Chapter II THE PROBLEM PROFESSOR

She didn't look so old herself. About twenty-two, Merritt estimated sardonically. If the young people of this age were destined to explore the planets, then she could be right in there pitching. But he liked her for knowing something.

The question most often asked him by people was, 'But

how can a ship fly in space where there's no air for the explosions to push against.' He saw that her enthusiasm was subsiding.

She said, 'Actually, that isn't what I meant when I asked you about your plans. What I want to know is what do you expect of Father?'

Merritt explained that they wanted the famous Professor Hillier, atomic bomb scientist, to be ready to go to Washington at the proper time to help persuade President Graham to support Project Spaceship. When he had finished, the expression on the girl's face was distinctly unhappy.

'Can't you,' she asked, 'obtain the support of some other scientist?'

Merrit said simply, 'We need a household name. Years ago there was Edison, then it was Einstein, now it's Hillier. You can't fight a thing like that. It's just so. Besides, some of the more famous atomic scientists will have nothing to do with the government since atomic energy was virtually placed under military control.'

He shrugged. 'Naturally, since no secret is involved, our members basically support the scientists. But we're willing to work with the material we have. We've found individual military men absolutely co-operative. They've given us German V-One and V-Two bombs.

'Jet and other planes have been turned over to us in almost any quantity we could ever hope to need. The armed forces are full of young eager officers and men who are only too anxious for somebody to reach the planets.'

His voice was warming to the level of enthusiasm. He realized suddenly that he was being boyish. He stiffened.

He said quietly, 'The world is as full as ever of the spirit of adventure. But people have to be cajoled and set on the right path to the future.'

'My father,' said Drusilla Julia Hillier, 'is going to be difficult. I'll be frank about that.' She went on earnestly, 'Mr Merritt, as you know, he was one of the atomic bomb scientists. After the war he visited Hiroshima and – well, it affected him.

'Norman and I have prepared a letter which we have already shown father, and which we are trying to persuade him to sign. So far he has not done so. I'm afraid it will be up to you to persuade him.'

The french windows opened and Lowery strode in. ' 'Lo Dru,' he said. He looked at Merritt. 'Sorry, I've been so slow but it's taken me all this time to locate the professor.' His voice had a peculiar note in it, as he added, 'will you come this way, and meet him in one of his favourite poses.'

The girl said, her colour high, 'Be seeing you at dinner, Mr Merritt.'

Merritt went out, puzzled. Outside he began in an irritated tone, 'For heaven's sake, Norman, what's going on here? This mystery is – '

He stopped. They had rounded a line of shrubs and there was a man lying on the grass under the trees. He was a gaunt old fellow with white hair, and a distinctively long head. His face was partly hidden by one arm. His expensive clothes were dishevelled and his posture twisted and ungainly.

As Merritt gaped in a gathering comprehension, Lowery said, 'Liquor has been unfair to Professor Hillier. It just wasn't meant for him. One or two glasses of the mildest concoctions and his whole system backfires like that. He's very determined, though. He's going to lick it yet, he says. Well, shall we go back into the house?'

Merritt went without a word. But he was thinking that getting a full-grown spaceship into the air was going to be more difficult than he had dreamed.

Professor Hillier came in to dinner. His eyes were quite bloodshot but he didn't stagger. He shook hands affably with Merritt.

'If I remember correctly,' he said, 'you came out and had a look at me. My daughter and her – ahem – I believe they're going to get married, but you never can tell about these moral young men – believe in letting visitors form their own conclusions. A very poor policy if you ask me. This world is too full of infidels and other non-drinkers.'

Merritt wasn't sure just what he ought to say.

Before he could speak Drusilla said, smiling, 'Father still lives in the era in which young people, when thrown together, automatically fall for each other. Norman and I have our own friends and personally I have yet to meet the man I am going to marry.'

Merritt glanced at his friend. Lowery was staring straight ahead with studied indifference and Merritt had his first realization of the situation that existed here. Boy loves girl but girl does not love boy. And the ass was making his situation hopeless by ageing under the strain.

They sat down to dinner. The professor said, 'Who's going to fly VB-Two?'

Merritt parted his lips to answer, then stopped himself, and looked at his host narrow-eyed. He couldn't have asked for a better question but after what he had heard of this man he'd have to take care not to let himself be drawn into a trap. He replied cautiously:

'The choice is between two men.'

He went on to explain the tests that had been given every member of the Rocket Club. The important thing was the ability to withstand acceleration. The army had several wonderful men whose anti-acceleration capacities were almost miraculous. Several of these had offered privately to perform the flight. But it had been decided not to use them for fear of arousing the ire of the high command.

'So,' Merritt concluded, 'we'll have to do it ourselves. A salesman, named John Errol, is the most likely man.' He saw that it would be unnecessary to name the second in line.

'What,' asked Professor Hillier, 'are your plans for getting to the President?'

Merritt was surer of himself now. At least he was getting a chance to explain. He said, 'The route is rather complicated. We have selected key men whose support we feel we must get before we can even approach the President. We want to interest a top brass hat in both the army and the navy.

'It happens that one of our members knows a high naval official who has practically guaranteed us support. But if the army should turn thumbs down it might stop us for years.

'However, all that is still more than a month away. We all agree that we must first obtain the support of Professor Hillier. Unless some famous scientist will say that space flight is possible it will be difficult to convince the so-called hard-headed businessmen.'

Professor Hillier was scowling. 'Businessmen!' he snarled, 'Yaah!'

Merritt thought: 'Oh-oh, here it comes.'

The professor had been eating with the concentrated intentness of a hungry man.

Now he paused. He looked up. His scarlet eyes gleamed.

91

'This desire to go to the planets,' he said, 'is the neurotic ambition of supreme escapists from life.'

His daughter looked at Merritt, then said quickly, 'That sounds odd, doesn't it, coming from a man who has made a fortune out of exploring the frontiers of science and who, moreover, has hung on to his money with the skill of a hard-headed businessman.'

She added, addressing her father directly, 'Don't forget, darling, you're committed to space travel. You're going to write a letter.'

'I haven't written it yet,' said Professor Hillier grimly. 'And I am toying with the idea of not writing it. The thought that a scientist in his cups might stop man from reaching the stars fascinates me.'

The conversation had taken a turn that Merritt did not like. He recognized in the professor a man who had tossed aside his inhibitions late in life. Such people always overdid their freedom. And that was a danger.

'Don't you think, sir,' Merritt said quietly, 'that it would be more fascinating if – uh, a scientist in his cups were the key figure in reaching the planets. Fact is, that's the only way it would ever get into the history books. It isn't history if it doesn't happen.'

Professor Hillier showed his teeth. 'You're one of these bright young men with an answer for everything,' he said. He made it sound offensive. 'Your attitude towards life is too positive to suit me.'

He put up a hand. 'Wait,' he thundered.

'Father really.'

The professor scowled at his daughter. 'Don't give me any of that really stuff. Here's a young man who rather fancies himself. And I'm going to show him up. Imagine,' he said viciously, 'pretending that he's an expert on space travel.'

He turned towards Merritt. He said in a silken voice, 'You and I are going to play a little game. I'm going to be a sweet old lady and you be yourself. You're cornered, understand, but very gallant. My first question is – '

He changed his tone. He was not a very good actor, so his tone was a burlesque and not very funny. 'But my dear Mr Merritt,' he said, 'how will it fly? After all, there's no air out there for the explosions to push against.'

*

Merritt told himself that he had to hold back his anger. He said, 'Rocket tubes, Mrs Smith, work on the principle that action and reaction are equal and opposite. When you fire a shotgun there is a kick against your shoulder.

'That kick would occur even if you were standing in a vacuum when you pulled the trigger. Actually, the presence of air slows a rocket ship. At the speeds a rocket can travel air pressure rises to thousands of pounds per square inch. In free space, away from the pull of gravity, a rocket will travel at many miles per second.'

'But,' mimicked Professor Hillier, 'wouldn't such speeds kill every living thing aboard?'

Merritt said, 'Madam, you are confusing acceleration with speed. Speed never hurt anybody. At this moment you are travelling on a planet which is whirling on its axis at more than a thousand miles an hour.

'The planet itself is following an erratic course around the sun at a speed of nineteen and a fraction miles a second. Simultaneoulsy the sun and all its planets are hurtling through space at a speed of twelve miles a second. So you see, if speed could affect you, it would have done so long ago.

'On the other hand you have probably been in a car on occasion when it started up very swiftly and you were pressed into the back of your seat. In short you were affected by the car's acceleration. Similarly, when a car is braked all of a sudden, everybody in it is flung forward. In other words, it had *decelerated* too swiftly for comfort.

'The solution is a slow gathering of speed. Let us imagine that an automobile is travelling at a speed of ten miles an hour, a minute later at twenty miles and hour and so on, ten miles an hour faster each minute.

'The driver would scarcely notice the acceleration but, at the end of a hundred minutes, he would be moving along at a thousand miles per hour. And he would have attained that speed by an acceleration on ten miles an hour per minute.

'Actually, human beings have survived decelerations – crash landings – approximating fifteen gravities. But it is recognized that the average person will be pretty close to death at six gravities and very few could survive nine gravities of acceleration.'

'What,' said the scientist, 'do you mean by gravities?'

'One gravity,' Merritt began, 'is the normal pull of earth

upon an object at ground level. Two gravities would be twice – '

At that moment he happened to glance at Drusilla, and he stopped short. She was white and Merritt realized that she thought he was following the wrong tack. He straightened.

He said, 'Really, sir, don't you think this is a little silly?'

'So you've got it all down like a parrot,' Professor Hillier sneered. 'Simple answers for simple people. Now the morons are going to learn about space and the planets and you're going to be the starry-eyed teacher.'

'The notion that everybody should automatically know all about your subject,' Merritt said, 'is a curious egotism in so great a man.'

'Aha,' said the professor, 'the young man is warming up at last. I suppose,' he said, 'you're also one of those who believe that the dropping of the atomic bomb was justified.'

Merritt hadn't intended to become angry but he was tired of the ranting of high and mighty moralists on the subject of the atomic bomb. And he was very tired indeed of the childishness of Professor Hillier.

'Well, sir,' he said, 'man lives partly with himself, partly with his fellows. Personally, I was an army pilot, and I'm assuming the dropping of the bomb saved my life. But in the meantime I have interested myself in the non-destructive aspects of atomic energy.' He shrugged. 'Materialistic. That's me.'

He took it for granted that he had lost the letter. But even if he had thought otherwise he was too wound up now to stop.

'Professor,' he said, 'you're a fraud. I've had a good long look at you and I'm willing to bet that you're never quite as drunk as you pretend. That business of spending half your time hanging on to the grass so you won't fall off the Earth is so fishy that I wonder you have the nerve to look anybody in the eye.

'As for all this nonsense about you having been strongly affected by the dropping of the bomb, you know very well that that was merely an excuse for you to turn your ego loose and – '

The professor had been stiffening. Abruptly, he glared at his daughter.

'Drusilla, you little Roman puritan, where's that letter you typed out for me to sign?'

'I'll get it,' she said hastily, rising.

'I'm going to sign it,' the scientist said to Merritt, 'and then I want you to get out of here before you ruin my reputation.'

A few minutes later, as Lowery was getting the car out of the garage, Professor Hillier came to the door where Merritt was waiting.

'Good luck,' he said, 'and happy planets to you, Mr Merritt.'

Chapter III MOUNTAINOUS MOLEHILLS

The partial victory had a heady effect on Merritt. By the time he got back to Los Angeles he was convinced that a letter was all he could have hoped for. He had Pete Lowery make fifty photostats and the huge pile that resulted made him glow. He phoned up Grayson, president of the Rocket Club, and reported his success.

He finished: '. . . and I'm leaving for New York tonight.'

'Oh, no, you're not,' said Mike Grayson. 'I was just going to call you and see if you were home.'

'What's up?'

It was a potential new member. Annie the superjet would have to be flown for his benefit and only Merritt and John Errol could fly the fast plane. Errol was out of town, so – Grayson's voice lowered in awe as he gave the final, important fact:

'It's for Rod Peterson, Bob.'

'The movie star?'

'None other.'

'What do you expect from him?'

They expected a ten-thousand dollar contribution. 'You know our policy. Each man according to his income. And our set-up is such that he can put it down as a bad investment on his tax declaration. Need I say the idea appeals to him?'

'What about *our* income tax?'

Grayson was complacent. 'We'll be on the moon before they discover that we're not paying any. Of course, in a kind of a way they recognize us as a non-profit organization but they're getting more and more suspicious, the silly asses.'

Merritt grinned. Contact with certain members of the Rocket Club always exhilarated him. The members in general moved through life as if they had wings in their hair, and a few of them imparted a special aura of the kind of intoxication that he himself had felt overseas.

Of all the millions of men who had built up an appetite for excitement they were the lucky ones who would be able to satisfy their desires. Without exception they had a conviction of high destiny.

Grayson finished, 'If we get the ten grand we'll give you one of them for your job. So you'd better be around.'

Ilsa merely sniffed when Merritt told her who would be at the barns. But later he found her dressing with minute care.

'It's time,' she said, 'that I took an interest in your work. And listen, you chump, when you climb out of the plane come over to me first. Then I'll be the starry-eyed wife hanging on to your arm when you're congratulated by Rod Peterson.'

Merritt always considered the drive over Cahuenga Pass into the valley where the club barns were located as one of the scenic treats of Los Angeles. He sniffed the air appraisingly, and found it satisfactorily dry and warm.

'Annie's built for that. I'll be able to push her up to eighty per cent of the speed of sound and stay pretty near the ground. We're going to turn on all her lights, you know, and make quite a night show.'

There were preliminaries. Merritt, who had endless patience, spent the evening tuning Annie for her flight. He saw Peterson's arrival from a distance, but the details were reported to him from time to time.

The star arrived in three cars, two of which were filled with friends. The lead car contained Peterson and a female who was more dazzling than all the rest put together. It was she who delayed the tour by asking scores of questions. When they came to the unfinished frame of VB-2, she peered at length into the drive nozzles.

'You mean to tell me,' she asked finally, 'that you make a rocket drive by having a narrow hole for the gases to escape through?'

'That's the general idea,' Grayson explained, 'though

there's a design that's slightly different for each type of explosive.'

'Well, damme,' said the young woman, 'if life isn't getting simpler all the time.'

She fascinated the entire membership but it was half past nine before Merritt (or anyone else apparently) learned her name. She was Susan Gregory, a new star, just arrived from Broadway. Beside her Rod Peterson was a cold fish. At a quarter to ten her enthusiasm began to wane notably.

'What's next?' she asked, in a let's-go-home-now-Roddy-darling voice.

Annie was wheeled out – Annie the sleek, the gorgeous – Annie of the high tail. Susan Gregory stared with dulled eyes.

'I've seen one of those before,' she said.

It was dismissal. The evening was over. Ennui had descended upon the spirit of Susan Gregory and, watching the descent, Rod Peterson showed his first real emotion.

'Tired, sweetheart?'

Her answer was a shrug which galvanized him. 'Thank you very much,' he said hastily to Grayson. 'It's all been very interesting. Goodbye.'

They were gone before most of the members grasped what was happening.

On the way home, Ilsa was as tense as drawn wire. 'The nerve of her,' she raged. 'Coming there like a goddess bearing gifts and then pulling that stunt.' Bitterly. 'You've heard the last of the ten thousand, I'll wager.'

Merritt held his peace. He felt himself at the beginning, not the end of temporary setbacks. And he had no intention of being gloomy in advance. By the time they reached their apartment Ilsa was deep in mental depression.

'You made a mistake marrying me,' she sobbed. 'I'm too old for insecurity and ups and downs.'

'At twenty-eight,' Merritt scoffed. 'Don't be a nut.'

But when he boarded the plane the following night she had still not snapped out of her mood. The memory flattened his ego. He arrived in New York in a drab state of mind. If Grayson hadn't suggested the Waldorf Astoria he would have gone uptown to a cheaper place.

The first businessman he contacted, a nationally known railway executive, listened to him as to a child, patted him on the back and promised to get in touch with him.

A textile giant, physically small and plump, kept him waiting for two days, then threw him out of the office verbally – 'Wasting my time with such nonsense!' An airline president offered him a job in his publicity department.

Merritt returned to his hotel room from the final failure, more affected than he cared to admit. He had expected variations of failure but here was a dead-level indifference. Here were men so wrapped up in their own day-to-day certainties that he had not even penetrated the outer crust of their personalities. At six o'clock that evening he phoned Grayson in Hollywood.

'Before you say anything,' Grayson said, when he came on the line, 'you may be interested to know that we have received ten thousand dollars from – guess who?'

Merritt refused to hazard a guess.

'Susan Gregory.'

That startled Merritt. But his mood remained cynical. 'Have you got a cheque or a promise?'

'A cheque. But with a string attached.'

'Huhuh!'

'She wants VB-Two named after her. And we thought – well, what the heck, ten Gs is ten Gs. You can't beat that kind of logic. One thousand of it is on its way to you by air. How does that sound?'

It was like a shot in the arm. With a fervour approaching animation, Merritt described his new plan of action. He had made a mistake in approaching the men cold. What was needed was an intermediary, either incident or human being, to bridge the gap.

Human beings lived in separate worlds. Business executives lurked behind special concrete-like barriers, where they hid themselves from commercially minded people like themselves. The problem was to get to the human being inside. In every man there was a spark of wonderful imagination. There he kept his dreams, his castles in the air, his special self.

Grayson interrupted at that point, 'That sounds beautiful theoretically. But what have you got in mind?'

Merritt hesitated but only for a moment. 'I'll need the

help of the local branch of the club.'

'Oh!'

There was silence. Merritt waited patiently. No one knew why the New York branch of the US Spaceship Society had never amounted to anything. It was one of those things. A synthesis of discordant personalities, a dividing into cliques tending to stultify and infuriate the brighter brains.

In history, when such divisive elements attained national power, civilization stood still for a generation or more. How to break artificially induced immobility or retrogression? Sometimes one man had been known to do it.

The trouble was that the Los Angeles branch was annoyed at New York and was not too eager to share the fruits of its efforts. Grayson's reluctant voice came on the wire.

'All right and I'll back you. Now what's your plan?'

'What I want,' said Merritt, 'is all the available information about these men. Then I'd like the use of an old jet plane. I'm going after Mantin first, since he actually kicked me out of his office, and this time I'm using imagination.'

The fortification that was Textile's Mantin was stormed that weekend when a jet plane apparently crash-landed within a hundred yards of his hunting lodge. The pilot, discovering that it would require twenty-four hours to repair the machine, was invited to remain overnight.

Bayliss, the air corporation man, was bombarded with ceramic and metal miniatures of various rocket bombs, each one accompanied by a message stressing the pure motives of the club. An ardent collector, he recognized some of the items as rare and valuable.

In Washington Senator Tinker, that sardonic glutton, finding himself the surprised recipient of a daily shipment of imported foods obtainable only in New York, grew curious and granted an interview to a persistent caller, named Robert Merritt.

And so it came to pass that a young man attended a certain very exclusive poker session, where the avergae age of the players was nearly forty years above draft requirements. Senator Tinker introduced him.

'Gentlemen, this is Robert Merritt.'

There was a grunted response. Merritt sat down and watched the cards being dealt. He did not look immediately at General Craig. He received two cards, an ace down and an eight up. The ace in the hole decided him to stay, though it cost him five dollars before everybody had stopped raising. His third card was an ace. He himself raised thirty dollars before the belligerent colonel next to the general stopped backing a jack and a nine with raises of his own. His fourth card was a nine, his fifth another ace.

Three aces was not a bad hand for stud poker. In spite of one of the aces not showing no one bet against him. Merritt raked in the chips. He estimated just a bit shakily that he had won about $275, and that these men played a game that was miles out of his class financially.

His first two cards in the next hand were the two of spades and the seven of hearts. He folded and for the first time took a good though cautious look at General Craig. The great man's publicized face was as rugged in real life as his pictures showed him.

The shaggy eyebrows were shifting as he studied the cards of his opponents. His gaze came to Merritt's cards, flashed up, then down again. It was as swift as a wink but Merritt retained an impression of having been studied by eyes as bright as diamonds.

As the hand ended, the general said casually, 'So it's me you're here to contact, Merritt?'

Merritt was shocked but he caught himself. 'General,' he said, 'you're a smart man.'

The older man said thoughtfully, 'Robert Merritt. Where have I heard that name before? Hmmmmm, Robert Merritt, Captain Air Force, nineteen Jap planes, Congressional Medal of Honour.' He looked shrewdly at Merritt. 'Am I getting warm?'

'Uncomfortably,' said Merritt.

He was not altogether displeased but he was also impressed. He recognized that he was in the presence of a man with an eidetic memory. He lost nearly six hundred dollars in the three hands that followed, most of it in the third hand when, in a sort of desperation, he tried to make two eights do the work of three.

When that hand was finished, General Craig said, What are you doing now, Merritt?'

It was direct but welcome. 'I'm secretary,' Merritt answered, 'of the Spaceship Society, LA branch.'

'Oh!' The general's eyebrows went up. Then he looked at Senator Tinker. 'You old Ssstinker you,' he said. 'Do you realize what you've done, bringing this young man up here?'

'Well, general,' drawled the senator, 'they tell me that your army boys have been putting the pressure on you from all directions about this spaceship business. I thought I'd slip somebody in the back door. What are you holding up the parade for anyway? Is the idea too big for you?'

The commander in chief growled, 'That kind of stuff is all right for young men but an old artillery man like myself can't afford to come out into the open until the time is ripe.'

'When will the time be ripe?'

'Let me think,' said the general. 'VA-Two went four thousand miles an hour. VB-Two is now under construction, and will be completed shortly. It is destined to carry the first human being ever to attempt to reach space itself.

'I would suggest you accept the secret offer made you by Lieutenant Turner. That young fellow's a physical whiz. If anybody can stand the extreme acceleration of your crude machine he can.'

The senator's grin was broader. 'General,' he said, 'you so and so. You're an old spacehound yourself. I repeat, when would you consider the time ripe?'

'When I'm called in. Under such circumstances I could prepare a report and read it to the President. He's not interested in printed material. Bad eyes, I suppose.'

'Then we've still got to convince the President?'

'Exactly. That's your problem. And now, Merritt, there's one question I want to ask you.'

'Yes, sir?'

The general was scowling. 'How in – can a ship fly in space where there's no air for the explosions to push against?'

Chapter IV OUT AND BACK

Said Serkel, 'Print is nothing but a painful sensation on the iris. Print convinces nobody of anything. If you want to influence nobody have your words published in memo, magazine or book form.'

He was a bright-eyed, dried-up little old man and Merritt stared at him in fascination. He sent a quick look towards

Senator Tinker, found no help in the big man's sardonic smile and so he faced the old fellow again across the poker table.

'Don't you think, sir, it depends on whether or not your favourite critic recommends the book?'

'The critics,' said Gorin Serkel, 'are like mounds of shifting sand on top of which publishers pile books. If they acclaim a book one week you can be certain that they will give their accolade the following week to another book of diametrically opposite viewpoint. Undoubtedly the two books together will fail to influence more people than they failed to influence separately.'

It seemed to Merritt that he had better produce his letter quickly. But he hesitated. They had found Serkel on the veranda of his country home and they were still standing halfway up the steps. Like salesmen, Merritt thought, with no prospect of being invited to sit down.

A little uncertain, Merritt took out the letter, and extended it. Serkel shrank back.

'Writing!' he said. He shrugged. 'You might as well start unbuilding your ship right now.'

'This letter,' Merritt urged, 'is from Professor Hillier.'

'The President,' said Serkel, 'cannot even be influenced by his own speeches once they are made and available only in printed form.'

'But how does the country continue to run?' Merritt protested. 'Surely, a mountain of documents crosses his desk every day.'

'Details, yes,' said Serkel. 'Administrative necessities and acts of Congress – that he tolerates in the same fashion that he accepts the American dollar as good money. But nothing new.'

He added with asperity, 'The President expects of his friends that they will not embarrass him by peddling schemes which he will almost assuredly have to turn down.'

He looked at Senator Tinker, then at Merritt. 'The solution seems very simple to me. Professor Hillier is a world-famous scientist. His name will get you a hearing. His presence will safeguard you from a quick exit.'

Merritt and Senator Tinker looked at each other. There was no question that Serkel was now giving them his most earnest counsel. The only thing they could do was to explain the impossibility of using Professor Hillier as a safeguard for anything.

It was a dangerous form of disillusionment because Serkel might avail himself of the opportunity to fade out of the picture finally and forever. Serkel was thoughtful when Merritt had finished describing the professor.

'So the publicized Hillier is a figment of the imagination, deadly to his own purposes when paraded in person and a flop at everything but adding and subtracting on a level approximating infinity.'

He straightened. He said curtly, 'Under the circumstances, gentlemen, I do not feel inclined to entertain your proposition. I – '

Merritt had watched it coming. As he stood looking at the former presidential adviser, a kaleidoscopic memory of the two months just passed flashed through his mind. Slowly the remembrance stiffened him.

He felt no sense of egotism but Serkel didn't seem to understand that the men who wanted his help were not just ordinary human beings. They were men with a mission. They *couldn't* back down or withdraw permanently from any forward position. Merritt gathered himself.

'I think, sir,' he said, 'that I have not made clear the potentialities of a letter. Professor Hillier, clothed in his ivory-tower reputation, verbally produced by an experienced persuader, can accomplish more than any stranger named Professor Hillier meeting a stranger named President Graham.

'It is my belief, furthermore, that you have not clearly realized the possibilities of a final great achievement to climax your long and famous career. So that you might better understand the situation I invite you to attend two weeks from now the most exciting experimental flight ever attempted by men. I think you owe it to the future of human kind to ensure that you at least see the first man to fly into space.'

Serkel's expression was suddenly more intent, thoughtful.

'One personality on the scene,' Merritt pressed on, 'funnelling the convictions of many minds through his own voice, might conceivably capture the attention of the President for the necessary minutes without requiring him to read a line.'

He saw that he had an audience again. Serkel sat down. He looked even more thoughtful. At last he said, 'You and your friend and the letter are invited to stay for the weekend.' He raised his voice. 'Mrs Ess.'

There were footsteps. A pleasant looking woman came out on to the porch. Serkel said, 'Gentlemen, my wife. Mrs Ess, tell Jane two extra dinners until further notice. Make yourselves at home, everybody.'

He stood up and disappeared into the house, mumbling something to the effect that, 'The economic aspects of the Keynes taxation theory do not merit the contempt they undoubtedly deserve. I must tell the President.'

At least that was the way it sounded to Merritt.

Merritt's purely personal crisis came like an atomic bomb out of the blue on the day of the test. At twenty minutes to two, with the flight scheduled to begin at two, a pale Mike Grayson hurried out of the barns and approached Merritt.

He said, 'Bad news! Lieutenant Turner just phoned. His superior officer, not knowing General Craig privately gave his permission to fly VB-Two, has refused him leave because of some miserable manoeuvres they're beginning tomorrow. I phoned John Errol but his office says they can't locate him – he's out somewhere on business. You were always the only other choice, Bob, so – '

Merritt's first thought was of Ilsa. Ilsa who would not understand, who would think that he had once more lightly placed her future in jeopardy.

'We could postpone it,' said Grayson, anxiously.

Merritt knew better. There were men waiting in the observation hut who had come to this test for a variety of reasons. It was almost a miracle that they were present at all. No one was so aware as he that that miracle would not be easily repeated.

'No,' he said quietly. 'Naturally, I'll do it. But first I want to call my wife.'

His call went unanswered. He let the phone ring for several minutes, then hung up, disturbed. Ilsa had decided not to come to the test.

'Somebody's going to get killed,' she had said, 'and I don't want to be around when they bring in the body.'

It was an unfortunate remark.

The four-jet carrier plane, which was to take the rocket on

104

the first leg of its journey, took off without incident. It climbed like a shooting star but it was only about halfway up when the pilot's voice sounded from the earphones which were embedded in the cushions beside Merritt's head:

'Grayson wants to talk to you, Bob.'

Grayson was exultant. 'Bob, Serkel just phoned from Washington. As you know, he decided not to come to the test because he doesn't believe in melodramatic shows. Well, he had lunch with the President today. And he's done it, Bob. He's done it.'

The other man's enthusiasm seemed remote to Merritt. He listened to the details with half his mind, agreed finally that it was more important than ever now that the test be successful, and then put the matter out of his mind.

The pilot's voice said, 'Ready, Bob?'

'Ready,' said Merritt.

The ship turned downward into a power dive. All four of its jet engines thundering, gathering speed, it went down to twenty-five thousand feet, then twisted and zoomed upward at more than five hundred miles an hour.

'Now,' said the pilot tensely.

Merritt didn't see the door in the rear of the plane opening. But he felt the movement as the rocket slid backward through the opening. Then he was in bright sunlight. Through the treated, tinted plexiglass of the tiny cabin he had a glimpse of the dark sky above.

For two seconds the long shiny tube continued to fall. It was not really falling. Its upward speed was about three hundred miles an hour. It was falling, however, with respect to the carrier ship and the time gap was designed to let the big machine get away.

The process was electronically timed. Tick, tock, tick, tock – WHAM! He had tensed for it and that was bad. It was like being hit in every bone and muscle and organ, that first titanic blow of the rockets.

Merritt crumpled into the cushions and the springs below and around him. He had a dizzy glimpse of the big converted bomber falling away into the distance. In one jump it retreated from gianthood to a tiny dot barely visible in the haze of sky below. It vanished.

WHAAAAMM! The second blow was more sustained.

His head started to ache violently. His eyes stung. His body felt as if it weighed a thousand pounds. *It did.* The second set of explosions was designed to exert peak acceleration. But the speed of the rocket was probably still under 2000 miles an hour.

'Bob!' Grayson's voice. On the radio.

'Yeah!' The word came hard.

'Shall we go on?'

It hadn't struck him that they might abandon the flight if he didn't react well. Curiously that brought fury.

'Blast you,' he shouted. 'Get going.'

The explosions were radio-controlled and the third was a duplicate of the second. His body took it hard, harder than anything he had ever imagined.

He found himself puzzling blurrily about what had happened to the cushions and the springs. He seemed to be standing on a slab of metal with steel-hard metal braces pressing on to his arms and legs. Was that what happened to cushions under pressure?

It was tremendously dark outside. His vision was not clear but he could see dots of stars and, over to one side, a fiery blob. It took a moment to realize that it was the sun. He waited, cringing, for the fourth and last series of explosions.

He thought, 'Oh, Lord, I can't take it! *I can't!*'

But he did. And, strangely, the blow seemed less severe as if in some marvellous fashion his being had adjusted to its environment of violence. The series of blows pulsed rhythmically through his bones and attuned to his nerves.

'Bob!'

He was so intent on his own thoughts and feelings that it didn't strike him right away that he was being addressed.

'Bob – ' earnestly – 'are you all right?'

'Bob,' he thought. Bob?, that's me. Impatience came.

'Why, of course I'm all right.'

'Thank goodness!' The words were a whisper. And in the background, behind Grayson's voice, there was a murmur of other voices. '. . . Good man!' . . . 'Oh, wonderful . . .' Then once more, Grayson.

'Bob.'

'Yes?'

'According to the duplicate instruments down here, you're now six hundred miles up, and going higher at the rate of seventy miles a minute. How do you feel?'

He began to feel fine. There was no sense of movement now. His stomach felt kind of hollow but that was the only sensation. He floated in emptiness, in silence and darkness.

The stars were pinpoints of intense brightness that did not twinkle or glitter. The sun, far to his left, was only superfically round. Streamers of flame and fire mist made it appear lopsided and unnatural.

As Merritt blinked at it the sun came past him and turned away to the right. He watched it amazed, then realized what was happening. The rocket had reached its limit. Held by Earth's gravity, it was turning slowly, twisting gradually, falling back towards Earth.

Merritt said quickly, 'How high am I?'

'Eight hundred and four miles.'

It was not bad. He had topped the farthest limits of the atmosphere by more than three hundred miles. He had looked out at empty space – through protected plexiglass to be sure – but looked. Soon he would have to start thinking of getting clear of the tube, which was destined to fall into the ocean.

At forty thousand feet above sea level he set off the explosion that knocked the cabin free of the main tube. At fifteen thousand feet he bailed out of the cabin. His parachute opened at five thousand feet. He came down in an orange grove and walked to a filling station. The attendant charged him fifty cents for using the phone to call Grayson.

He was back on Earth all right.

The physical check-up at the field was extremely thorough and it took a long time. When it was over there were toasts and congratulations. It was nearly seven when Merritt reached the apartment.

He came in, carrying a bag of groceries, but it was evident that Ilsa had been shopping too. The pleasant odour of roast beef came from the kitchen.

A paper with screamer headlines about the flight lay on a French chair. The sight relieved Merritt. She knew.

Ilsa came out of the kitchen. She was smiling. 'How do you feel?' she asked.

'I've been pronounced one hundred per cent.'

She clung tightly to him as she kissed him but that was her

only show of emotion. 'I'll have dinner ready in a minute,' she said.

While they were eating Merritt told her, with more excitement than he had originally felt, about Serkel's success.

'The President,' he said, 'has assigned six thousand dollars for the development of an atomic drive for spaceships.'

'Six thousand dollars!' said Ilsa.

The colour went out of her cheeks. 'It that *all* he got. Six thousand dollars!' she exclaimed. 'Why, in Congress, members each session vote hundreds of thousands of dollars for each other's pet schemes without even knowing what they are.

'And you people are getting a wretched six thousand dollars to build a spaceship, a tribute no doubt –' furiously – 'to the fame of Professor Hillier. That's about the smallest amount the government has ever used for the brush-off.'

Merritt protested, amazed, 'But you don't understand.'

'I understand only too well. It's the same story all over again – no money.' She was so agitated she couldn't go on. Tears started to her eyes. She shook her head in frustration and hurried out of the room.

Merritt thought, 'Well, I'll be a –'

He went on under his breath, 'But you *don't* understand, Ilsa. According to Serkel the President was aware that it was a historic occasion. So he symbolized it. He assigned exactly the same amount of money that the atomic energy project had first received. It was like saying unlimited funds would be available.'

Merritt sat, eyes closed, tremendously disturbed. If he told her now it would be a case of buying back her love. He remembered suddenly that she had divorced her first husband just before the man struck it rich. He had a vision of her doing it again – and knew that he couldn't let it happen.

Footsteps sounded. Ilsa came back into the room, straight over to him. She buried her face against his knees.

'Bob, I couldn't help it. When I thought of you taking that terrible risk for nothing –'

She climbed to her feet and sat down on his lap. 'This will sound melodramatic,' she said, 'but this afternoon I swore to myself I would never again mention money to you.'

Merritt hugged her. 'That,' he said, 'is silly. There's something wrong about a woman who doesn't drive her husband.'

'You're a wretch,' Ilsa said cosily. 'But I still love you.'

'Good,' Merritt said.

He kissed her neck to hide his broadening smile.

Later, he would tell her that men would soon fly in atom-powered spaceships, first to the planets, then to the far stars.

THE INVISIBILITY GAMBIT

Written in collaboration with E. Mayne Hull

The big man came aboard the space liner from one of the obscure planets in that group of stars known as the Ridge.

The Ridge is not visible as such from Earth. It lies well to the 'upper' edge of the Milky Way; and the long, jerky line of stars that compose it point *at* Earth, thus showing as a little, bright cluster in an Earth telescope. Seen from Kidgeon's Blackness, far to the right, the Ridge stands out beautifully clear, one of the more easily distinguishable guidemarks in our Galaxy.

The area is not well serviced. Once a week an interstellar liner flashes down the row of stars, stopping off according to advance notices received from its agents on the several score little-known planets. On reaching the edge of the Ridge, the ship heads for the central communication centre, Dilbau III, where transfer is made to the great ships that traffic to distant Earth.

The entire trip requires about three weeks; and anyone who moved around as much as I did, soon learned that the most interesting part of the journey is watching the passengers who get on and off at the way ports.

That's how I came to see the big man as soon as I did.

Even before he came aboard from the surface craft that had flashed up to where we lay about a hundred thousand miles above the planet, I could see that the new passenger was *somebody*.

It was his luggage, case after case of it being hoisted by the cranes, which gave that information. Beside me, a ship's officer gasped to a fellow officer:

'Good heavens, that's ninety tons of the stuff so far!'

That made me straighten up with interest. They don't allow freight on these liners; and ninety tons makes up a lot of personal belongings. The officer spoke again:

'It's the permanent move, looks like to me. Somebody's

made his pile, and he's going home to Earth. Look! It's Jim Rand.'

It was.

I have a little theory of my own about legendary men of space like Jim Rand. It's their reputations that enable them to accomplish their greatest and most widely publicized coups.

Initial momentum is necessary, naturally, and boundless energy and courage, but that only makes millions. It's reputation that pushes such men into the billion stellor class.

Jim Rand's deep, familiar voice broke my reverie: 'Hello, there,' he said. 'I believe I know you, but I can't place you.'

He had stopped a few feet from where I stood, and was staring at me.

He was a man of about fifty, with a small moustache, and a nose that looked as if it had been broken, and then repaired under emergency conditions. That slight twist in it didn't hurt his looks any, rather it added a curious strength to the muscular lines of his face. His eyes were blue-green, bright now with puzzlement.

I knew exactly how he was feeling. People whom I've met, and meet again later, always wonder whether or not they know me; and sometimes they become very exasperated with their memories. It's up to me, then, to recall the occasion. Sometimes, I do that; sometimes I don't.

I said now: 'Yes, Mr Rand, I was introduced to you by a mutual friend when you were organizing the Wild Mines of Guurdu. Your mind was probably on more weighty matters at the time. My name is Delton – Chris Delton.'

His gaze was curiously steady. 'Maybe,' he said finally. 'But I don't think I'd forget a man of your appearance.'

I shrugged. They always say that. I saw that his face was clearing.

'Will you meet me in the lounge in about an hour?' he said. 'Perhaps we can talk.'

I nodded. 'Happy to.'

I watched him walk off along the brilliantly lighted corridor, redcaps wheeling several trunks and bags after his tall, powerful form.

He did not look back.

Beneath my feet I could feel the shudder of engines. The

great ship was getting under way.

'Yes,' said Jim Rand an hour and a half later, 'I'm through, I'm retiring, quitting for good. No more wildcat stuff. I've bought an estate; I'm going to get married, have some children and settle down.'

We were sitting in the lounge, and we had become more friendly than I had thought possible. The great, glittering room was practically deserted, nearly everybody having answered the first call for dinner.

I said: 'I don't wish to seem a cynic, but you know the old story: All this out here, these untamed planets, the measureless wealth, the dark vastness of space itself – it's supposed to get into a man's blood.'

I finished as coolly as I could: 'Actually, the most important thing in your life at the moment is that at least two, possibly four, men have been watching you for the past three minutes.'

'Yes,' said Jim Rand. 'I know. They've been there since we came in.'

'Do you know them?'

'Never saw them before in my life.' He shrugged. 'And I don't give a damn either. Five years ago, even last year, I might have got myself excited about the possibilities. Not now. I'm through. My mind is made up. I've laid my plans.'

He settled back in the lounge chair, a big, alert man, smiling at me with a faint, amused expression in his eyes.

'I'm glad you were aboard,' he said, 'though I still can't remember our last meeting. It would have been boring alone with all these little minds.'

He waved a great hand with a generous gesture that took in half the ship. I couldn't suppress a smile. I said:

'Boredom – there'll be plenty of that on Earth for a man of action. The place is closed in by the damnedest laws – all kinds of queer regulations about not carrying energy guns – and if anybody bothers you, or starts trouble, you've got to settle it in court. Why, do you know, they sentence you to jail simply for owning an invisibility suit?'

Rand smiled lazily. 'That won't bother me. I gave all mine away.'

I stared at him, frowning. 'You know,' I said finally, 'I've found that trouble never asks whether it's welcome or not.

112

Don't look now, but somebody's just got out of the elevator, and is coming towards you.'

I finished: 'If you need any help, just call on me.'

'Thank you,' said Jim Rand. He smiled his lazy smile, but I could see the gathering alertness in him. 'I usually handle my own trboule.'

It was I who had the vantage point. I was facing the elevator. Rand was sitting sidewise to it; and, superb actor that he was, he did not deign to glance around, or so much as flick an eyelash.

I studied the stranger who was approaching without looking at him directly. His eyes, I saw, were dark in colour, rather close-set behind a long, thin nose. It was a wolfish face thus set off, with thin, cruel lips and a receding chin that yet gave no suggestion of weakness. The man eased his lank body into the lounge beside Rand.

Ignoring me, he said: 'We might as well understand each other.'

If Rand was startled by that, there was no indication on his face. He smiled, then pursed his lips.

'By all means,' he said. 'Misunderstandings are bad, bad.'

He clicked his tongue sadly, as if the memory of past misunderstandings and resultant tragedies was passing through his mind. It was magnificently done, and I could not restrain a thrill of admiration.

'You are meddling in something which is no business of yours.'

Rand nodded thoughtfully to that, and I could see that the movement was more than an actor's gesture. It must be occurring to him by now that he had better put some thought to such an open threat.

His voice was light, however, as he said: 'Now, there, you have touched on one of my pet subjects – business ethics.'

The man's dark-brown eyes flamed. He spat his words: 'We have already been compelled to kill three men. I am sure, *Mr* Blord, you would not want to be the fourth.'

That startled Rand. His eyes widened; and there was no doubt that he was shocked at the discovery that he was being mistaken for someone else, particularly *that* someone.

I don't know whether I'm qualified to speak about Artur Blord. He's simply one of several dozen similar types of men who made the Ridge their stamping ground. Cities spring up where the heavy hand of their money points. And that brings more money, which they concentrate elsewhere.

Blord differed from the others only in that he was a mystery, and few people had ever seen him. For some reason this added to his reputation, so much so that I have heard people speak about him in hushed whispers.

The shock faded from Rand's face. His eyes narrowed. He said coldly:

'If there must be a fourth dead man, I assure you it won't be me.'

The wolf-face man actually changed colour. That's what reputation can do. He said hastily, his tone conciliatory.

'There's no reason for us to be fighting. There're nine of us now, all good men that even you, Blord, cannot afford to antagonize. I should have known I couldn't scare you. Here's our real proposition:

'We'll give you ten million stellors, payable in cash, *within an hour*, provided you sign an agreement stating that you will NOT get off this ship tomorrow at Zand.'

He leaned back. 'Now, isn't that a fair and square offer?'

'Perfectly,' said Rand, emphatically, 'perfectly fair.'

'Then you'll do it!'

'No!' said Jim Rand. And moved his right arm about a foot. It was a long distance for that powerful arm to gather momentum; and its effect was comparatively devastating.

'I don't like,' said Jim Rand, 'people who threaten me.'

The man was moaning, clutching at his broken nose. He stumbled blindly to his feet and headed for the elevator. His four companions gathered around him, and they all vanished into the glistening interior.

As soon as the elevator door closed, Rand whirled on me. 'Did you get that?' he said.' he said. 'Blord! Artur Blord is mixed up in this. Do you realize what it could mean? He's the biggest operator on this side of Dilbau III. He's got a technique for using other men that's absolutely the last word. I've always wanted to stack up against him but – '

He stopped, then hissed: 'Wait here!'

He walked swiftly towards the elevator, stood for a moment staring at the floor indicator of the machine the others had taken, then climbed into the adjoining lift. Ten minutes later, he settled softly in the seat he had left.

'Have you ever seen a wounded nid?' he said exultantly. 'It heads straight for home without regard to the trail it may leave.'

There was bright fire in his gaze, as he went on briskly: 'The chap whom I hit is called Tansey; and he and his gang have taken Apartments three hundred to three-oh-eight. The outfit must be new to the Ridge stars. Proof is they mistook a person as well known as I am for Blord. They – '

Rand stopped short there. He looked at me sharply. 'What's the matter?'

'I'm thinking,' said I, 'of a man who's retiring; his plans are all made, estate, wife, children – '

'Oh!' said Jim Rand.

The glow faded from his eyes. Some of the life went out of him. He sat very still, frowning; and I didn't have to be a mind reader to see the struggle that was taking place in his mind.

At last, he laughed ruefully, 'I *am* through,' he said. 'It's true I forgot myself for a moment, but I must expect occasional lapses. My will remains unalterable.'

He paused; then: 'Will you have dinner with me?'

I said: 'I had dinner served in my apartment before I came to meet you.'

'Well, then,' he persisted, 'how about coming up to my rooms a couple of hours from now?' He smiled. 'I can see you're sceptical about me, and so you may be interested in proof that I'm really in earnest. I've got the presidential suite, by the way. Will you come?'

'Why, sure,' I said. I sat watching him walk off towards the dining room.

It was half past eight – all these stellar ships are operated on Earth time – when Rand opened the door for me, and led me into his living-room. The whole room was littered with three-dimensional maps, each in its long case; and I was familiar enough with the topography that was visible to recognize the planet Zand II.

Rand looked at me quickly, laughed and said: 'Don't get any wrong ideas. I'm not planning anything. I'm merely curious about the situation on Zand.'

I looked at him carefully. He had seated himself; and he

115

seemed at ease, casual, without a real worry in him. I said, finally:

'I wouldn't dismiss the matter as readily as that. Remember, you didn't invite their attention in the first place; they're not liable to wait for future invitations, either.'

Rand waved an impatient arm. 'To hell with them. They'll be off the ship in fifteen hours.'

I said slowly: 'You may not realize it, but your position in relation to such men is different than it's ever been. For the first time in your existence, you're thinking in terms of your personal future.

'In the past, death was an incident, and, if necessary, you were ready to accept it. Wasn't that the general philosophy?'

Rand was scowling: 'What are you getting at?'

'You can't afford to take any chances. I'm going to suggest that I go to Apartment three hundred, and tell them who you are.'

Rand's gaze was suspicious. 'Are you kidding?' he said. 'Do you think I'm going to eat dirt for a bunch of cheap crooks? If I have to handle them, I'll do it my way.'

He shrugged. 'But never mind. I can see you mean well. Take a look at this, will you?'

He indicated one of the long map plates, on which showed a section of the third continent of the planet Zand II. His finger touched a curling tongue of land that jutted into the Sea of Iss. I nodded questioningly, and he went on:

'Last time I was on Zand, they were building a city there. It was mostly tents, with a population of about a hundred thousand, about three hundred murders a week, and atomic engineering was just coming in. That was six years ago.'

'I was there last year,' I said. 'The population then was a million. There are twenty-seven skyscrapers of fifty to a hundred storeys, and everything was built of the indestructible plastics. The city is called Grenville after – '

Rand cut me off grimly. 'I know him. He used to work for me, and I had a run-in with him when I was on Zand. Had to leave fast at the time because I was busy elsewhere and because he had the power.'

A thoughtful frown creased his face. 'I always intended to go back.'

I nodded. 'I know. Unfinished business.'

He started to nod to that. And then he sat up and stared at

116

me, I was absolutely amazed at the passion that flared in his voice, as he raged:

'If I went around finishing up all the business I've started and paying off all the ingrates, I'd still be here a thousand years from now.'

His anger faded. He looked at me sheepishly. 'I beg your pardon.'

There was silence. Finally, Rand mused: 'So there're a million people there now. Where the devil do they all come from?'

'Not on these liners,' I said. 'It's too expensive. They come packed into small freighters, men and women crowded together in the same rooms.'

Rand nodded. 'I'd almost forgotten. That's the way I came. You'd think it was romantic to hear some people talk. It's not. I've had my skinful of frontier stuff. I'm settling in one of the garden cities of Earth in a fifteen-million-stellor palace with a wife that will – '

He broke off. His eyes lighted. 'That's what I want to show you,' he said. 'My future home, my future wife.'

Rand led the way into the second sitting-room – the lady's sitting-room, it's called in the circulars – and I saw with surprise that he had had a screen fitted up against a wall and there was a compact projector standing on the table.

Rand switched off the lights and turned on the projector. A picture flashed on the screen, the picture of a palatial house.

The first look made me whistle. I couldn't help it. They say that men don't dream of homes, but if ever anything looked like a dream come alive, this was it. There was a flow in the design, and a sense of space. I can't just describe that. The mansion actually looked smaller than it was; it seemed like a jewel in its garden setting, a white jewel glittering in the sun.

There was a click; the picture faded from the screen, and Rand said slowly:

'That's the house, built, paid for, fully staffed. Am I committed, or am I not?'

In the half darkness, I said: 'It can't possibly cost more than a million stellors a year to maintain. Say, another million to operate a space yacht and to cover the overheads of watching your holdings. Your share of the Guurdu

Mines alone will pay for it all ten times over.'

A light blinked on; and I saw that Rand was glaring at me. 'You're hard to convince,' he said.

'I know the hold,' I said, 'that the Ridge stars get on a man.'

He leaned back, relaxing. 'All right, I'll admit everything you say. But I'm going to show you something now that you can't set up against a money value.'

He reached towards a table on which lay some X-ray plates. I had noticed them before. Now, Rand picked up the top one and handed it to me. It was of a woman's spine. Beside it, on the plate was written in some species of white ink:

Dear Jim:

The most perfect spine I have ever seen in a woman. When you consider that her IQ is 140, the answer is: don't let her get away. With the right father, her children will all be super.

KARN GRAYSON, M.D.

'It that the woman?' I asked.

'That's she.' I could see that he was looking at me sharply, studying my face. 'I've got more plates here, but I'm not going to show them to you. They simply prove that she's physically perfect. I've never met her personally, of course. My agents advertised discreetly, and among all the trashy women who answered was this marvel.'

In my life, in conversation with strong men, I've never been anything but frank. 'I'm wondering,' I said steadily, 'about the kind of woman who sends her specification like a prize animal.'

'I wondered about that, too,' said Jim Rand. 'But I'll show you.'

He did.

There will always be women like Gady Mellerton, I suppose, but not many. They're scattered here and there through time and space; and each time the mould is destroyed, and must be painstakingly re-created. Invariably, they know their worth, and have no intention of wasting themselves on little men.

On the screen, she seemed tall, about five feet six, I

118

judged. She had dark hair and – distinction. That was the essence of her appearance. She looked the way a queen ought to look and never does.

Her voice, when she spoke, was a golden, vibrant music:

'All I've seen of you, Jim Rand, is a picture your agent gave me. I like your face. It's strong, determined; where you are you're a man among men. And you don't look dissipated. I like that, too.

'I don't like being up here, parading myself like a show horse. I don't like those X-rays that I had to have taken, but even in that I can appreciate that, far away as you are, you must set up standards and judge by them. I'm supposed to describe my life, and I like that least of all.'

Click! Rand cut off the voice, leaving the picture. 'I'll tell you the rest,' he said.

He told me about her, as I sat there unable to unloose my gaze from the screen.

'She's a multi-operator. That's one of those damn jobs out of which you can't save any money. I don't mean that the salary isn't good. But they grab a piece out of it for old age insurance, for sickness, for compulsory holidays, and so much for clothes a year, so much for housing, entertainment. You've got to live up to your income. You know the kind of stuff.

'For the people as a whole, it's paradise, a dream come true, but the only way a woman can break out of it is to marry somebody. Actually, when a first-rater gets caught in one of those perfect jobs, she's sunk. It's the purest form of slavery. It's hell with a capital H. Can't you just picture it?'

I said nothing. I sat there looking at the woman on the screen. She was about twenty-five; and I could picture her going to and from work, on her holidays, swimming. I could picture the beautiful children she would have.

I grew aware that Rand was pacing the floor. He seemed to realize my unqualified approval, for he was like a little boy who has shown off a new, remarkable toy. He glowed. He grinned at me. He rubbed his hands together.

'Isn't she wonderful?' he said. *'Isn't she?'*

I said at last, slowly: 'So wonderful that you can't afford to take any chances with her future. So wonderful that I'm going to loan you an invisibility suit, and you're going to sleep on the floor tonight.'

Rand paused in his pacing, confronted me. 'There you go again,' he scoffed. 'What do you think I am, a little sissy? I'm not hiding from anybody.'

His arrogance silenced me. If I had been asked at that moment whether Jim Rand was heading straight for Earth, my answer would have been an unqualified 'yes.'

It was an hour later when we separated, and nearly two hours after that when my doorbell sounded. I answered at once. Jim Rand stood there.

He looked startled when he saw that I was fully dressed. 'I thought you'd be in bed,' he said, as I shut the door after him.

'What's the matter?' I asked. 'Anything happen?'

'Not exactly.' He spoke, and he did not look straight at me. 'But after I went to bed I realized that I'd been very foolish.'

My mind leaped instantly to the girl, Gady Mellerton. 'You mean,' I said sharply, 'you're not going to Earth?'

'Don't be silly.' His tone was irritable. He sank into a chair. 'Damn you, Delton, you've been a bad influence on me. Your crass assumption that I'm lost if I deviate in the slightest degree from my purpose actually had me leaning over backward, suppressing all my normal impulses, my natural curiosity, even my mental approach to the subject. That's over with. There's only one way to deal with their type of person.'

I offered him a cigarette. 'What are you going to do?'

'I'd like to borrow that invisibility suit you mentioned.'

I brought the two suits out without a word, and offered him the larger: 'We're much of a height,' I said, 'but you swell out more around the shoulders and chest. I've always used the big one when I'm carrying equipment.'

I saw his gaze on me oddly, as I pulled the second suit over my clothes. 'Where do you think you're going?' he said coolly.

'You're heading for Apartments three hundred to three-oh-eight, aren't you?'

'That's right but – '

'I feel sort of responsible for you,' I said. 'I'm not going to let that girl be stuck in her job, or be forced to marry some tenth-rater because you get killed at the last minute.'

Rand grinned boyishly. 'You sort of like her looks, eh?

OK, you can come along.'

Just before he put on his headpiece, I brought out the glasses. I said: 'We might as well be able to see each other.'

For the first time, then, since we had met, I saw Jim Rand change colour. He stood for a moment as if paralysed; and then his hand reached gently forth and took the glasses. He stood there with them in his fingers, staring as at a priceless gem.

'Man!' he whispered finally, 'man, where did you get these? I've been trying for fifteen yeras to get hold of a pair.'

'There was a shipment,' I said, 'of five dozen to the patrol police on Chaikop. Four dozen and twelve thousand stellors arrived. I figured they were worth a thousand apiece.'

'I'll give you,' Rand said tensely, 'ten million stellors for this pair.'

I could not for the life of me suppress a burst of laughter. He scowled at me, snapped finally:

'All right, all right, I can see you won't sell. And besides you're right. What the devil does a family man want with them on Earth anyway!' He broke off. 'How well can you see with them?'

'Pretty good. Help me switch on the lights. That'll give you a better idea.'

It's really startling how little is known about invisibility suits. They were invented around 2180, and were almost immediately put under government control.

Almost immediately. It was soon evident that someone else was manufacturing them secretly, and selling them at enormous prices. The traffic was eventually suppressed on all the major planets, but it followed the ever receding starry frontiers, its sale finally limited by a single fact:

Only one man in a hundred thousand was willing to pay the half-million stellors asked for an illegal suit.

The cost of manufacture, I have been told, is three hundred stellors.

Try and suppress that kind of profit. Fifty years have shown that it can't be done.

The strangest thing about the suits is that they work best in bright sunlight. Come twilight, or even a dark cloud, and the wearer takes on a shadowy appearance. In half darkness, a suit is practically worthless.

When the power is switched off, an invisibility suit looks

like a certain type of overalls extensively used for rough work. It takes a very keen eye to detect the countless little dark points of – not cloth – that make up the entire surface.

Each one of these points is a tiny cell which, when activated, begins to absorb light. The moment this occurs the cell goes wild. The more light turned on it, the wilder it becomes. The limiting factor is the amount of light that is available.

That was why I had the lights switched on in my apartment, so that Jim Rand could look at me under conditions where, without the glasses, I would have been completely invisible to him.

It was day-bright in the big hallway, too. These enormous ships always try to give the impression of sunniness even in deepest space. It's supposed to be good psychology. No one with an invisibility suit could ask for a better light.

As I closed the door of my suite, I could see Rand just ahead of me, a shimmering shape. His suit glittered as he walked, and took on strange, shining light-forms. It blazed with shifting points of colour, like ten thousand diamonds coruscating under a brilliant sun.

It was the sleeping hour; and the long corridors were empty. Once, a ship-officer passed us, but both Rand and I were accustomed to the curious sensation of watching a man walk by with unseeing eyes.

We reached Apartment 300. I used my key of ten million locks – and we were in. All the lights were on inside, and a man lay on the living-room floor, very still. It was one of the men who had been watching Rand in the ship's lounge. Not the leader, Tansey.

Automatically, Rand floated off like a god of light into the bedroom. I headed for the bathroom, then the spaceroom. When I came back, Rand was kneeling beside the man.

'Been dead,' he whispered to me, 'about an hour.'

He began to go through the fellow's pockets, pulling out papers. That was where I stepped forward, and put a restraining hand on his wrist.

'Rand,' I whispered, 'do you realize what you're doing?'

'Eh?' He looked up at me. His face showed as a blurred pool of light, but even in spite of that I could see the surprise in it. 'What the devil do you mean?'

'Don't look any further,' I said. 'Don't try to find out any more.'

His low laughter mocked me. 'Man, are you harping on that again? For all I know, in a minute I'll find out from these papers what this is about.'

'But don't you see,' I said earnestly. '*Don't you* see – it doesn't matter what it is. It's simply another big Ridge deal; it can't be *more* than that. You know that. There have been thousands like it; there'll be millions more.

'It may be a new city; it may be mining, or any one of a dozen other things. *It doesn't matter.*

'Here's your test. You can't leave half your soul on the Ridge and take half with you. For you, it's all or nothing. I know your type. You'll always be coming back, ruining your life and hers.

'But if you can stop yourself now, this minute, this second and go out of here, and dismiss the whole affair from your mind – '

He had been listening like a man spellbound. Now, he cut me off brutally:

'Are you crazy? Why, I'll lie awake nights from sheer curiosity if I don't find out what this is, now that I've been dragged into it.'

His voice took on an arrogant note: 'And suppose I do get off at Zand tomorrow, and stay for a few weeks. Am I a slave to the idea of retirement? It was never my intention to be anything but free to act as I pleased. I – '

'*Ssshh!*' I said. 'Here comes somebody.'

Rand stood up in a leisurely fashion, the true sign of the experienced invisible man. No quick movements! Soundless action. We stepped back from the body as near the door as possible.

It was in such moments that the glasses were priceless. Ordinarily, in a crisis, two invisible men working together are a grave danger to each other's movements.

The door opened, and four men came in, the last of them being Tansey. He had a white bandage on his nose.

'Price was a damned fool,' he said coldly. 'He should have known better than to try to murder a fellow like that. Just because we received the eldogram from Grenville telling us that he'd never sent that other message, he – '

Another man cut him off: 'The important thing is to slip him into this invisibility suit and dump him through the refuse lock.'

They trooped out into the empty corridors, carrying their invisible burden.

When they had gone, Rand said slowly, grimly: 'So Grenville's in on this – '

I stood at the great entrance lock, watching the ship cranes load Rand's baggage on to the surface craft that had soared up from Zand II.

The planet rolled below, a misty ball of vaguely seen continents and seas, a young, green, gorgeous world.

Rand came over and shook my hand, a big man with a strong, fine face. I couldn't help noticing the way his hair was greying at the temples.

'I've eldogrammed Gady,' he said, 'that I'll be there in two or three weeks.'

He saw the look on my face, and laughed. 'You must admit,' he said, 'that the opportunity is one that I can't afford to miss.'

'Don't kid me,' I said, 'you don't even know what it's all about.'

'I will,' he said, smiling. 'I will.'

I knew that.

His last words to me were: 'Thanks for the loan of the suit and glasses. That cuts you in for twenty-five per cent of anything I make.'

I said: 'I'll see that my agents contact you.'

I watched his big form move off through the lock. Steel doors clanged between us.

As soon as the ship started to move, I went to the purser's office. He looked surprised.

'Why, Mr Delton,' he said, 'I thought you were leaving us at Zand.'

'I changed my mind,' I said. 'Book me through to Earth, will you?'

That was three years ago.

My wife is looking over my shoulders as I write this. 'You can at least,' she says, 'explain.'

It's really very simple. When I saw Rand come aboard, I

eldogrammed my agent on Zand II. He sent a message to Tansey, purporting to come from Grenville, describing Rand, and stating that the man of that description was Artur Blord, who, the eldogram said, must be prevented from landing.

Rand reacted the way I expected. The only thing was, when I saw the girl, I changed my mind. I had my agent wire Tansey that a mistake had been made and that Rand was – Rand.

Tansey grew suspicious, and wired Grenville, who disclaimed all knowledge of the previous eldograms. At this point Price came to my suite to kill me. I used the large invisibility suit to cart his body to Apartment 300; and it was still lying there when Rand and I entered.

The reason I interfered in the first place with Rand's purpose of retiring was because I wanted to use him to force my interest into the tremendous uranium find that had been made on Zand. I've found that I become bored with the actual details of organizing a great mining development, and I do it only when I can't find a man to whom such details are life's blood. A man who will moreover let me buy in in some fashion.

Naturally, I used my knowledge of the psychology of spacemen. It's clear to me now that, once those kinds of forces are set in motion, they can't be stopped.

I looked up at my wife. 'Well, Gady,' I said, 'will that do?'

'Except that like a good sport, Mr Rand sold us the house.'

Gady insisted on calling our first-born by my full name: Artur Christopher Blord Delton.

You see, Rand convinced me. A man has to retire some time.

REBIRTH: EARTH

Written in collaboration with E. Mayne Hull

The white crescent of moon flitted from cloud to cloud, as if it, too, was a great, three-engined plane charging high above the night waters of the northern Atlantic.

Twice, when its shape was partly hidden by a wool-pack of a cloud, the illusion of another plane with all lights on was so vivid that Squadron Leader Clair stiffened, fingers instinctively reaching for the radio switch, and words quivering on his lips to warn the silly fool out there that this was war, and that, within half an hour, they would enter the danger zone.

Reflections, Clair muttered the second time, damn those reflections of that bright, glowing moon.

In the half light, he turned to Flying Officer Wilson, but, for a moment, so dazzling was the play of moon rays through the domed glass cockpit that – for that prolonged instant – the navigator's body seemed to shine, as if a million glittering reflections were concentrated on his long, powerful frame.

Clair shook his head to clear his vision, and said: 'Never saw the moon so bright. Puts one in mind of the old folks' tales about the power of the moonbeams to conjure shapes, to reflect strange things that do not exist – '

His voice trailed. He squinted at the man beside him. With a tiny start, he saw that it was not Wilson, but one of the passengers. The fellow said in a quiet voice:

'How goes it?'

It was not the words themselves, but a suggestive quality in the tone that, for a moment, brought to Clair a pleasant kaleidoscope of memory: his famliy home on the lower St Lawrence, his mother, tall and serene, his calm-eyed father, and his younger sister soon to be married.

He shook the picture out of his brain a little irritated; they

126

were private possessions, not to be shared by any chance interrogator. Besides, here was merely some faint heart requiring reassurance about the flight.

'Everything's fine!' Clair said; and then in a precise voice, he added. 'I'm sorry, sir, passengers are not allowed in the cockpit. I must ask you to – '

For a second time, then, he stopped in the middle of a sentence, and stared.

It was hard to see the man's face; the moon made a dazzling, reflecting fire where it splashed against his skin and body. But what Clair could make out against that surprising glare was finely constructed, a strangely strong, sensitive countenance with grey eyes that smiled a secret smile, and gazed steadily, expectantly, across at him. A tremendously interesting face it was, only –

It was not the face of any one of the passengers.

With a gasp, Clair ran his mind over the passengers, as he had checked them in hours before. Typical, they had been, two dozen of them. A sprinkling of diplomats, a little troop of military men, and a faded group of civil servants, including one government scientist.

He remembered them all, vividly, and this man had not been – Beside him, the stranger said quietly:

'I wish to report my presence aboard your ship!'

'You . . . WHAT?' said Clair; and his amazement was all the more violent because his mind had already led him to the very verge of the truth.

The man made no reply, simply sat there smiling quietly – and the moon, which had momentarily flashed behind a cloud, jerked into sight again and rode the dark-blue heavens to the south-southwest.

The light shattered into blazing fragments on the cockpit glass, and cascaded like countless tiny jewels, bathing the stranger in a shield of radiance.

Swiftly, Clair drew his mind into a tight acceptance of the situation that was here. His eyes narrowed; his face took on a stern expression. When he finally spoke, it was the squadron leader, commander of men, who said curtly:

'I have no idea why you have chosen to stow yourself on this ship, nor do I desire any details. It is my duty to place you in irons until we land in England.'

With a flick of his hand, he drew his automatic – as the cockpit door opened, and vaguely silhouetted the bulky figure that was Wilson.

'Queerest thing that ever happened to me, Bill,' the flying officer began. 'One second I was sitting beside you, the next I was lying in the baggage compartment. I must have walked in my sleep and . . . oh!'

His eyes glinted steely blue in the moonlight, as he sent one swift glance at the gun in Clair's fingers, then flashed his gaze to the stranger.

'Trouble?' he said, and snatched his own gun.

It was the stranger who shook his head. 'No trouble at the moment,' he said. 'But there is going to be in a half an hour. They've found out about your cargo, and the attack will be in force.'

He finished softly: 'You will need me then.'

For a single appalled moment, Clair blanched. 'You know about our cargo!' he said harshly; and then, dismayed by his own admission, snapped:

'Flying Officer Wilson, you will take this man to the baggage room, search him, and put the irons on him. If he goes quietly, keep your gun in your pocket. No use alarming the passengers unnecessarily.'

'I shall go quietly,' said the stranger.

Almost disconcerted by the man's acquiescence, Clair watched him being led through the moonlit cabin. The affair seemed unsatisfactory – unfinished.

Ten minutes later, the first distant streaks of dawn tinted the long, dark waters to the east; but the crescent moon was still master of the sky. Clair sat at the controls, his forehead twisted into a worried frown. Only occasionally did he glance at the flying shape of light that, for so many hours now, had flooded the night and the sea with its brilliance.

His brow cleared finally. Because – there was nothing to do but carry on. He turned to Wilson to say something to that effect; the navigator's voice cut off his words:

'Bill!'

With a start, Clair saw that his friend was gazing with a tensed fixedness into the mirror that showed the long, dimly visible passenger cabin. His own gaze flicked up, strained against the quiet gloom that was out there. But there was nothing.

The moon glowed in through the dozen windows, probing at the passengers with soft fingers of light. Some of the men were sleeping, heads nodding low, their faces shadowed by their posture. Others sat talking; and their countenances, too, made patterns of light and shade, that shifted, as they moved, into a thousand subtly different umbral effects.

It was a restful scene, utterly normal. A puzzled question was forming on Clair's lips, when once more, urgently, Wilson spoke:

'The third seat from the back – the fellow leaning across the aisle talking to Lord Laidlaw, the British diplomatic agent – it's *him*.'

Clair saw. Very slowly, he stood up. He had no real sense of abnormal things. 'Take the wheel, sir,' he said. 'I'll go see what's what.'

Wilson said: 'I'll keep an eye on you.'

As Clair squeezed out into the passenger cabin, the stranger looked up. It seemed impossible that the fellow was able to see him, where there were only shadows, where the moonlight did not penetrate, but he must have. He smiled, said something to his lordship, and then stood up.

Clair's fingers flashed to his gun, then relaxed, as the man turned his back, and, walking to the rear of the aisle, sank into a double seat that was there.

Once more, he looked up, seemingly straight into Clair's eyes. He beckoned Clair to the vacant seat beside him. The squadron leader approached hesitantly. There was something very strange here, but his mind wouldn't quite hurdle over the strangeness.

He loomed over the man, then, frowning, sank down beside him. He said curtly:

'How did you break out of those irons?'

There was no immediate answer; and, for the thousandth time in that long flight, Clair grew conscious of the intense brilliance of the moon. Crescent-shaped, it raced high in the heavens to the south-southwest; and it did shining things to the broad, dark belly of the sea. The water seemed as near as

129

the night, and, like ridges of glass, sent up a shadowed blaze of reflection.

Reflections that caught his eyes, and made it preternaturally hard for him to look intently at the stranger, as the man said:

'I didn't think you would believe me if I told you that the irons would be useless against me. Accordingly, I am letting the fact speak for itself.'

Clair made an impatient gesture. He felt a genuine irritation at the other for talking nonsense now, when the zone of danger was so incredibly near.

'Look here,' he snapped, 'it is within my authority to put a bullet in you if I consider that your presence will endanger this ship. Who are you?'

'Let me understand you,' the man said, and his voice was curiously troubled. 'You see nothing unusual in the fact that I *have* broken out of the irons?'

'Obviously,' said Clair, 'you're one of those people with very small hands.'

'I see.' The man was silent; then: 'This is going to be even more difficult than I imagined. I thought that my escaping from your manacles would release you to a small degree from your normal mental inhibitions.'

'What are you talking about?'

'I'm afraid,' was the strangely sad reply, 'I'm afraid you wouldn't understand. If I could convince you, I would tell you my identity, but your mind is too enthralled by the practical world in which you have your being. By a trick, by means of a moon-ray time reflector machine, I have established my existence in that world, and now you accept me. But I am afraid I shall have to plan my purpose around that limited fact. I had hoped you would free all my enormous strength but – '

He broke off, then finished: 'Your friend searched me, and found no weapons; therefore you should not object to letting me sit here till the destroyer planes come – even under the terrible handicap of your reality, I think I can save you then.'

Clair had listened to the unfolding words with the growing, empty conviction that he was talking to a madman. Now, for a moment, he cursed silently the incredibly bad luck that had forced such a situation upon him in this, his most important flight. He began angrily:

'I don't know what kind of nonsense you've got in your mind, but I'll tell you this much: if a flight of Messerschmitts attack us in the next forty minutes, our machineguns won't be much good. In any event, they'll be manned by Flying Officer Wilson, Colonel Ingraham and Major Gray. If you have some queer idea that you – '

He cut himself off decisively: 'I'm afraid I have no choice, but to put the irons on you again. They're adjustable, and this time I'll see that they don't slip off.'

The man nodded gravely, and, without a word, led the way back to the baggage compartment –

Returning forward, Clair paused beside Lord Laidlaw. He said: 'For your private information, sir, the man to whom you were talking a minute ago is a stowaway. I would like to ask you what he said to you.'

His lordship was a plump-faced man with keen, greyish eyes. He fixed them shrewdly on the squardon leader. 'Funny chap,' he commented finally. 'Had a hard time seeing him because of the way the moon kept shining in his face. I'm afraid his remarks were very trite, though they stirred some pleasant memories and generally titillated the idealistic side of my nature. He asked me how it went with me and my family.'

Frowning, Clair strode on to the cockpit.

The light in the east was stronger; a world of greying shadows that streaked the grey-dark waters; and all the horizon glowed with that first faint promise of a brilliant morning.

Some of the ice began to thaw out of Clair's mind; the new lines of worry in his forehead smoothed, and an eager expectancy crept into his eyes.

'Well – ' he finished the low-voiced discussion with Wilson – 'we're agreed. I've already set the ship in its new course. If anyone is seeking a rendezvous with us on the basis of secret knowledge of our planned course, they'll have to look again. I – '

He stopped, as the cockpit door tilted open, and the semibald head of Lord Laidlaw was outlined in the gloom of the door's shadow.

'Er,' said his lordship, 'that fellow has come back into the

131

passenger cabin. You said you had put him in irons, so I though I'd better mention it.'

Clair spun out of his seat. 'By God!' he flared, 'that fellow's hands mustn't actually be any larger than his wrists. He's been selected for this job, and I'm going to find out what it is.'

His fury sustained him, as he hurried along the aisle. But it died abruptly as he paused, and stood, frankly nonplussed, staring down at the fellow. The vague wish came that the moon would go behind a cloud, so that the might get a really good look at the interloper.

Before he could narrow his complex thoughts into words, the stranger said in an astoundingly stern voice:

'I hope you have sufficient imagination to be convinced that you cannot imprison me. I assure you that time is short.'

Clair sank down in the seat beside the other. 'Look here,' he said in his most reasonable voice, 'you don't seem to realize the seriousness of your actions. Now tell me, how *did* you get out of those irons?'

Through the unnaturally radiant reflections of the crescent moon, Clair saw that the stranger was staring at him steadily. The man said finally, slowly:

'Squadron Leader Clair – you see, I know your name – I am aboard this ship to save it from what will be, without my aid, certain destruction. There are two ways in which I can do that. The first is, if you remain ignorant of my identity and allow me, when the enemy comes, to operate one of your machine-guns. This is by far the best method because it involves no mental contortions on the part of you or your passengers. You simply continue to accept me automatically as a physical entity. Do anything you please to protect yourself; keep pistols trained on me – anything: but in the final issue, do not try to stop me from using a machine-gun.'

'Look here – ' Clair spoke wearily – 'you've already undermined my career simply by being aboard. I'll have to explain my negligence in not discovering you before we took off, and I can just see myself adding that I substituted you for Colonel Ingraham on one of the machine-guns.'

He stared at the other with earnest conviction in his mind that he was persuading an unbalanced person.

'I'm putting it that way,' he said, 'so that you will see my side, and realize the impossibility of your request. You've got some idea that we have a valuable cargo aboard. You're mistaken. You – '

He had intended to turn again to persuasion, but a new thought brought him to frowning pause: If he could slowly change the subject and – He said swiftly:

'By the way, what *do* you think we have aboard?'

The man told him quietly; and Clair changed colour. He sat for a moment as still as death, all purpose forgotten before the tremendous fact that the man actually did know. Then, white and grim, he said:

'I admit it's a valuable load, but only in the narrow sense of the word. Its value is little more than a hundred thousand dollars. I can't see the German Air Command wasting time trying to trap a plane whose take-off time they could not possibly know, especially when their interceptor planes would be so much better occupied trying to sink the ships of that convoy we passed half an hour ago.'

He grew aware that the stranger was staring at him with a melancholy sardonicism. The man said:

'Squadron Leader Clair, there has never been a more valuable cargo shipped. Its destruction changed the course of world history.'

'*Its destruction!*' echoed Clair; then he caught himself. He gathered the realities of his situation back into his brain. There was no longer any doubt: here beside him was a raving madman and – The man was speaking again:

'In searching me, your friend refrained from removing a book which is in my right coat pocket. I had this book printed under great difficulties in what used to be New York City; and I would like you to glance at page twenty-seven, and read there part of the description of the flight of this ship, and what followed when it was shot down, and lost with all on board.'

Clair took the book, and there was not a thought in his head, as he stared down at it. There was a feeling in him that he was dreaming; and the unreal effect was augmented by the way he had to bring the book close to his eyes, and hold it just so to let the moonlight fall on it.

Page twenty-seven, he saw, was heavily underscored. The first paragraph, so marked, read:

'The three-engined transport, NA-7044, left its New-

133

foundland airport at 9.00 p.m., 26 November, and was shot down at 4.12 a.m. the following morning, both times being Greenwich, and in the year AD 1942, which was in the curious, old chronology. The chief pilot was Squadron Leader Ernest William Clair, a very practical and conscientious young man. The passengers included Thomas Ahearn, admiralty agent, John Leard Capper, American government physicist, Lord Laidlaw, who was returning to England after having failed in his mission to –'

Clair tore his gaze from the page; his thought scurried madly back to the phrase that had struck him like a blow. 'God God!' he gasped. 'Where did you get that plane number? No one knew definitely which plane was going out until late last night.'

'You poor fool!' the stranger said sadly. 'You still think in terms of your reality. If you continue so blind, there is no hope.'

Clair scarcely heard. He was jerking up his wrist, peering at the watch that was strapped there. He felt a strange heady shock, as he saw the time.

It was exactly three minutes after four.

For Clair, the strange thing in that tensed, startled moment was that he became aware of the throbbing of the engines. The sound, so long subdued by familiarity that it scarcely ever touched his consciousness, was a whine that sawed along his nerves. His brain twanged with that poignant and ceaseless roar.

Through the fury of the beating motors, he heard himself say coldly:

'I don't know what your game is, but the very elaborateness of your preparations proves that the most drastic measures are in order. Therefore – '

He paused wildly, stunned by the dark and deadly intention in his brain: to shoot, not to kill, but to incapacitate.

The stranger's voice cut across his stark hesitation:

'All this that you have seen and heard; and it means nothing to you. Does your mind simply reject the very intrusion of a new idea? What is there about Good that, at certain stages of its development, it falters, and stands trembling and blind on the edge of the abyss, while Evil ablaze with a rejuvenated imagination, strides to its dreadful victory?

'I can see now that for he, here, success in the great way is impossible. But try, try to lift your mind above this binding sense of duty and – let me handle the machine-gun. Will you promise?'

'No!' Clair spoke with the distinct finality of one who was utterly weary of the subject. Squadron Leader Ernest William Clair, DFC, went on: 'You will refrain from further attempts, please, to embellish on this fantastic story. When we reach England, I shall have you arrested as a spy, and your explanation will have to be very good indeed if you hope even to account for what you have already revealed. It will be assumed – and it is you who will have to prove otherwise, that your purpose aboard this ship was destructive and – '

His voice faded. Clair swallowed hard, and the thought that came was like a black tidal wave that swept him to his feet with a cry. He drew his gun, and backed hastily along the aisle, holding it tense.

From the corners of his eyes, he saw heads jerk up, and passengers twist in their seats. He had their attention, and he said swiftly, in a clear, ringing voice:

'Gentlemen, we have a stowaway aboard; and, as I am unable to obtain a coherent story from him, I must assume that he might have smuggled a bomb aboard. He keeps repeating that this ship is to be destroyed within fifteen or twenty minutes – the exact hour he mentions is twelve minutes after four – so it could be a time bomb.

'*Hunt for that bomb!* Everyone, out of your seats! This is no time for niceties. Down on your knees, search every corner, every compartment – and someone scramble into the tail. Use flashlights, but keep them pointed at the floor. Now, hurry!'

An officer with a deep voice said quietly: 'Sirs, let us make this thorough. Civilians and military are about equally represented aboard. The civilians take the rear, the soldiers the front.'

Clair added swiftly: 'I suggest a cursory search of one minute, followed by a detailed examination. Is that satisfactory, Colonel Ingraham?'

'Excellent!' said the colonel.

It was the strangest thing in the world, standing there in that swift, darkened plane, half watching the shapes of the men, as they crawled around, peering under seats, poking into bags, examining racks – half watching the stranger, who sat like a graven image, face turned into the flood rays of the moon, which was farther to the rear of the ship now, its strong, refulgent light pouring in through the windows at a distinct angle.

The man said slowly, without bitterness, but with infinite sadness:

'This futile search, when all you have to do is to look in your own minds. The seeds of your destruction are there. If this ship is lost, freedom goes with it. There are no other key points in our time. Once more: will – you – let – me handle that machine-gun?'

'No!' said Clair; and there was silence between them in that hurtling, moonlit ship.

The white moonlight made a network of dim light, casting long shadows across the dark cabin, doing distorting things to the straining faces of the men, as they searched. Flashlights glowed cautiously at brief intervals, peering into dark corners, glaring hard against shiny surfaces.

Three – then five minutes; and they were all back in the cabin. They formed a dark cluster around Clair, where he stood, his revolver trained on the interloper. Their faces, out of the direct line of moonlight that streamed through the faintly shuddering windows, formed a series of roughly circular light splotches.

Only the stranger was in the light, and he was silent. Clair explained briefly what had happened, and what precautions he had taken; he finished:

'So you see, we had him in irons twice; and each time he came out here. Did you examine them, Lord Laidlaw, when you were in the baggage room, as I suggested?'

'Yes,' The nobleman spoke briskly. 'They were still locked. I should say that we have here one of those curious people who can contract their palms to the size of their wrists.'

'In my opinion,' said Colonel Ingraham, 'this man is mad. The story he told you is definitely that of an unbalanced

136

person. The solution is to put the irons on him *out here*, and have him under guard till we land.'

'There's one point,' interrupted a very clear, incisive voice. 'This is Ahearn speaking, by the way, Thomas Ahearn of the admiralty – one point: You mentioned that he showed you a book, and that it contained – what?'

Clair handed the volume over quietly. 'If you'll bend down towards the floor,' he suggested, 'you can use your flashlight on it.'

Men pushed past him to get around the admiralty man; then a light gleamed; then –

'Why, it contains some queer account of the flight of this plane, with all our names.'

'Is my name there?' came a new voice from the back of the mass. 'Brown – Kenneth Brown!'

'Yes, it's here.' It was Ahearn who answered.

'But that's impossible!' Brown ejaculated. 'I didn't know until two hours before we left that I would be on this plane. How could anybody find that out, write it up, and publish a book about it – and, for Heaven's sake, why would they want to?'

Clair stood very still; and the queerest feeling came that he was listening to his own voice saying these shallow, useless words, making protests about the impossibility of it all, crying out to the idolatrous god of logic with a parrotlike fanaticism, and never once *thinking* about – anything.

He glanced automatically at his watch, tensed a little, and said tautly:

'Gentlemen! If you will allow me, I shall ask the prisoner one question.'

It took a moment for silence to settle, but he needed the time to frame the incredible question that was in his mind. He said finally:

'Stranger, when did you come aboard this ship? I said – when?'

The man's eyes were steady pools; his face grew noticeably more distinct. 'I heard you, Squadron Leader Clair. To you alone, for your consideration, I say: I came aboard about forty minutes ago. Think of that; think it through; don't let it go.'

Exclamations blurred across his last words; then Colonel Ingraham snapped angrily:

'Sir, we haven't time to bother with this person. Let us iron him, and set a guard over him.'

Clair's brain was like rigid metal. The stiff feeling came that he ought to turn and apologize to the others for his utterly ridiculous question. But there was a fascination in his mind that held him spellbound; and finally a thought that was a twisting, irresistible force; he said:

'What is your real reason for being aboard this ship?'

The reply was a shrug; then: 'I'm sorry; I see I was mistaken about you. I've already told you in effect that this is a key flight in history. It *must* get through; it can only get through with my help.'

He shrugged again, finished: 'I notice that you have shifted the course of the ship. That is good, that is something. It has already broken the hard trail of events, and the attack will be delayed. But that delay will be small – out of all proportion to the extent of your change of course. Seven, eight minutes at most.'

For a second time, Clair was silent. The thought came that the shadows of the early morning and the dazzling, crescent moon were affecting his mind. For incredibly, he was not rejecting a single word; for him, for this moment, this man's every word formed a species of reason and –

And, he'd better be careful; or he'd be out of the service for being a credulous fool. He, whose nickname at training school had been Solid-head Clair, *credulous!*

So swiftly came revulsion. He shook himself, and said, striving for coldness:

'Now that we have verified that there are no bombs aboard, I think Colonel Ingraham's suggestion is the best: In irons, under armed guard, out here. Colonel Ingraham and Major Gray, I suggest you man the machine-guns to which you were previously assigned – '

His voice trailed off, for the stranger was staring at him with bitter anguish.

'You blind fool. I can only exist if you sustain the illusion that is me with your minds; and that illusion would collapse instantly if I had to sit out here in chains, under guard. Accordingly, I must leave; and the first hope, and the best, is gone. Now, you must *know* my identity. When you need me, call – but there will be no answer unless you call with understanding. Good-bye.'

For an instant, so determinedly did Clair's mind refuse to accept the absence of the form that had been there, that he blinked.

Then the thought came that the moon was too bright, and that dazzling reflections of its white, too white rays were playing tricks with his eyes. And then –

Reality penetrated the absence, the utter absence, of the stranger.

They searched the ship, as the dawn in the east grew noticeably stronger, casting its pale, wan glow over all the sky ahead and all the forward sea. Only the west behind them remained dark; and the moon was there, a shining, hurtling shape, yielding not yet to the brightness of the new day.

And it was exactly four twelve by the glowing hands of Clair's wristwatch, as the men grudgingly gave up their vain search.

'Funniest thing that ever happened!' a voice tilted against the dimness. 'Did we dream that?'

'I could swear he dived for the floor just before he vanished,' said a second voice. 'He must be somewhere. If we could shift some of that baggage – '

'At least – ' it was the man, Brown – 'we've still got his book.'

Twelve minutes after four.

Clair raced along the aisle to the cockpit. 'Anything?' he said to Wilson. 'See anything – any planes?'

He stared with Wilson, and with Major Gray, who was at the port machine-gun, into the brightening world. But there was nothing, not a speck, nothing but the sky and the sea and the – moon!

It glittered at him, and hurtled along through the blue-dark heaven; and the thought came to Clair: the silvery crescent moon – creating – reflections –

4.14 a.m.

And he felt no relief; for he *had* changed the course, and the man had said it would mean only infinitesimal delay.

Minutes, and then – bullets crashing into them all, a terrible fusillade that would burn and tear and destroy the whole world – unless –

Unless he called with understanding of identity! But how could he ever understand? There were no clues, nothing but a scatter of meaningless words, nothing but – death.

A man whose hands flicked out of handcuffs, who talked of key points in history, who had a book that described this flight, and the destruction of all on board, described it as a past event. The book –

He was out in the dimness that was the cabin. 'The book!' he called. 'Who's got the book that chap left?'

'Right here,' said the man, Kenneth Brown. The passengers were all in their seats. 'I've been reading out passages. Damnedest, queerest book I ever laid eyes on. It's actually got my name in it –' he couldn't seem to get over the wonder of it – 'my name, imagine that. You've got to give these Germans credit –'

The funny thing, Clair thought – no, the incredible tragedy of all this, was that their minds wouldn't accept what their eyes had seen. Something shaped like a human being had come into their midst, then vanished before their eyes – and their brains simply skittered over the impossible event; and now they sat here like so many spectators who had been entertained by a magician, wondering in a thrilled, unworried fashion how the devil the trick had been worked.

Danger, the black and deadly danger – they saw it not. But blindly chattered on about everything except the reality.

'Show him the frontispiece!' A voice cut into his burning reverie. 'That's the real give-away. It's in German.'

The man, Brown, echoed: 'Absolutely, the whole frontispiece in German. Look, the name of that city.'

The book was held up into the light of the moon; a shadowed finger pointed. Clair strained and read:

Zweiundvierzigste Strasse
Hitlerstadt, Nord-Amerika
743 N. H.

'What gets me,' said Brown, 'is that seven-four-three N. H. at the bottom. It's senseless.'

Clair said greyly: '*Nach Hitler*' – it was funny how he knew, but he did, with utter certainty – 'after Hitler. Seven hundred and forty-three years after. Hitlerstadt is, of course,

140

the city we now call New York.'

There was a ripple of laughter, and somebody said: 'Wha' did he say? Wha' did he say?'

The sentence was repeated, but the man did not echo the laughter. 'Oh,' he said, 'Oh, I'm glad somebody's got a sense of humour. I've just been sitting here thinking if this might not be some manifestation of a secret enemy weapon. And I must say, I couldn't think of how they could have worked it.'

There was more laughter. It was amazing to Clair how good-humoured they had become. Somebody whispered to him: 'That's Capper, the scientist.'

'I know!' Clair nodded. He was thinking desperately: If he could keep them thinking it was all humour, and yet gain information – He said, straining for lightness, but heavy and cold with the import of his words:

'Professor Capper, we might as well carry this through: Is there a theory of time which would explain how an event which has already occurred can be changed, so that something entirely different would transpire?'

'Of course, of course.' The scientist spoke irritably. 'The world is full of nonsensical ideas. Everything's been thought of – everything. Trust human beings to waste their time with such stuff.'

Clair fought an inner battle to keep his fingers from grabbing the other's neck, and shaking the explanation out of him. The sense of urgency in him was so great that his voice trembled as he said:

'For the sake of curiosity, what is the theory?'

'Why, it's nothing but the old factor of – '

The plane swerved in a dizzy, twisting dive that sent Clair hurtling against a seat. He caught the plush back of the chair with a grip that nearly tore his muscles from his body.

There followed a sickening moment where the only sound was the shrill whine of the engines in the full fury of a power dive; and then –

Glass splintered. Bullets smashed against shiny woodwork, and screeched on metal. From somewhere near, a man screamed in the agony of death. Clair cursed aloud with a terrible understanding. The great transport plane had been swept from tail to nose by machine-gun fire.

*

He managed to wedge his body into the comparative stability and safety of the seat opposite the scientist, Capper – and through the window he saw the silver-thin planes of the crooked cross, black pencils against the lightening sky.

Three of them darted past his narrow line of vision, like black angels gleaming in the moonlight, reflections of malignant beauty –

The thought came to Clair that he ought to be struggling to reach the cockpit, and that he was ruining himself by sitting here, ruining his great record, ruining himself in the eyes of the passengers.

Ruin – utter ruin –

And it mattered not. The thoughts were in his mind, but they were like burning phantoms, consuming their own substance, completely uncorrelatable to physical action. In his brain was one purpose, one unquenchable and tremendous purpose.

He leaned over to the scientist; he half shouted:

'What is this theory of time?'

He braced himself for a verbal explosion, a tongue-flaying that would sear his brain; an opinion about an officer neglecting his duty that would sting in his memory throughout all time. And there was a picture in his mind, a vivid, terrifying picture, of how the question he had asked would sound in court-martial testimony.

It mattered not. All the certainties, the motivations that had ruled his brain in the past seemed remote and unreal. There was only –

'Professor Capper, that time theory of which you spoke?'

'Young man,' came the reply, 'you amaze me; your courage, your calmness – Thank you, sir, for being so matter-of-fact. Your example saved me from making a cowardly fool of myself. But I'm under control now – and you're right, there is no reason why we shouldn't discuss science or pseudoscience – '

Clair stared blankly; then came a brief, dark sound at the other's unexpected reaction. It was a form of hysteria, of course; and there was ego here, an utter acceptance that a plane commander would, in a crisis, waste his time talking to a passenger. But –

For *his* purpose, it was as if God Himself had reached

forth His magic hand, and rendered everything easy. Fighting for control, Clair said:

'Professor, the time theory – give it to me as succinctly as possible.'

'A lot of nonsense, of course,' the man rumbled, 'but fascinating to talk about under such conditions. Probable worlds! Imagine that – '

His voice trailed off; Clair heard him muttering something more about nonsense – and trembled so violently that he could hardly stay in his seat.

'Probable worlds? What do you mean?'

'What I said. Suppose the ancient Sea-peoples had conquered Egypt; suppose Xerxes had defeated the Greek States; suppose the Moors had overrun Europe; suppose the Germans won this war; suppose – '

'But how does that fit the theory?'

In the light of the moon, the thin face of the professor frowned at Clair: 'Don't be so impatient. There is no hurry. The attack isn't over yet; and we might as well talk. I want to thank you again for making it possible for me to face this situation with a fearlessness I never expected was in me. It feels great, wonderful. It – '

The twisting thought came to Clair that he would have to tell this loquacious *savant* the truth. He parted his lips – and then, through the window, he saw the black shape swoop in from the north.

'Duck!' he yelled, and jerked himself flat on the aisle floor, as the plane crackled and reverberated with the bullets that tore along its length.

A heavy body collapsed on top of Clair. At least, it felt unbearably heavy at the moment of fall; only it was surprisingly easy to lift the professor's slight form back into his seat. The man crouched there, coughing a little, mumbling to himself.

Cold with the certainty of what had happened, Clair shook the drooping body.

'Professor – '

The head lifted wearily; and a strong glow of moonlight reflected from a pair of small, watery eyes.

'Never so proud,' came the mumble. 'Never thought I'd face death like this. How can we lose the war, if even I – '

'The time theory!' Clair croaked.

'Oh, yes, the old business of probables – You're the bravest man I ever met, squadron leader, to carry on such a conversation; and I'm not so bad myself. Tell them that, eh? Tell them we talked about . . . about time theories, about worlds and men that might have existed if – something hadn't happened. Of course, to the theorist, those worlds do exist, that is, some projection of them, something of the spirit that carried on – '

'Professor, that stranger – he claimed to be from the future that would exist if we won this war – '

For an instant, after Clair had spoken, the scientist's watery eyes brightened; he mumbled: 'So that's what you've been getting at. But it's impossible. I'll tell you why – if he was only from a probable world, he couldn't have materialized here.'

'But he didn't materialize. That's what he said. That's why he could slip out of our irons. He was only a reflection of – and this is his own phrase – of a moon-ray time reflector machine, and that we had to accept the illusion mentally before it would even exist as much as it did. Professor – '

'Impossible. You've forgotten the book he left. That was material.'

'But, sir – ' Clair had a hopeless feeling – 'he said he had that printed under great difficulties in Hitlerstadt.'

'Spirit – ' the professor's voice was a remote, husky thing; and it was all too obvious that his mind had gyrated back to an earlier theme – 'that's it, spirit like ours cannot die . . . proud that I personally took a bullet without flinching, and after all my fears, too . . . proud – '

He crumpled like a house of cards; and Clair who had seen death too often to doubt its presence now, climbed over the contorted body in the aisle. He was shaking a little, but his mind was quite clear. Whatever hope there might have been of some mysterious superman coming to the rescue from a world that had yet to prove its right to exist – that hope was gone now.

The only man who knew enough to fill in the all-necessary details of identity was dead, and that meant –

The time had come to fight.

The two men in the cockpit snarled at him like beasts as he entered. Clair saw, from narrowing eyes, that Wilson's right

144

arm hung, a limp, tattered, bloody object at his side. Major Gray was at the port gun, hugging it to his shoulder. Both men flashed him the desperate expressions of human beings determinedly facing a hopeless martyrdom. It was Wilson who raged:

'Where in hell do you think you've been, you damned – '

There was, Clair recognized in a biting self-condemnation, justice behind those lashing words. But they were born of maddening pain, and served no useful purpose. He knew exactly what to do, what to say; his answer grew *alive* out of events:

'Silence!' He flared the words, because only anger could penetrate here. He sneered: 'So you've given up in your hearts, both of you. Think we're licked eh? Going to go on shooting to the last, but deep in your minds you know it's all hopeless. What can a transport do against fighter planes?

'Shut up!' He snapped the words at Major Gray, whose lips were parting for speech. 'I know exactly what you're thinking, but I've just seen a man die, who knew how, and if anybody in this cockpit disgraces him, I'll take that person's body, and throw it out of the ship. Only men are going to have the honour of going down with this plane.'

Before that blazing tirade, the two men, Wilson and the major, exchanged one amazed glance. Gray shrugged his stocky shoulders with the unmistakable gesture of a man who recognized stark insanity when he saw it.

Clair didn't feel mad. His whole body was aglow with life that quivered like an itching finger on a hair trigger. Never had he been more alert, more conscious of the utter joy of being.

He saw the torpedo-shape silhouette for an instant against the moon, and as the Messerschmitt dived towards them in a long, slanting curve, he crouched over the starboard gun, his mind rock-steady, his whole body intent on aiming.

After a moment, he compressed the trigger gently, and held it back.

It took a moment, then, for his eyes to recover from the blinding light that ballooned into incandescence where the Hun ship had been.

A shrill yell sounded from Wilson: 'Good boy! He blew up!'

The remote thought came to Clair that men in crises were

chameleons in their emotions. His navigator who had hated with violence, now praised in a storm of approval.

That thought passed because – he noticed the oddness with a start – there was a difference in the feel of the gun. It was bulkier. But it felt strangely, immensely lighter; immeasurably easier to handle.

But there was something else, a mind-soaring difference: it had glowed green against the half light of the early morning sky; the whole shiny barrel had tinted a pale, iridescent green.

And the funniest part of all was that he had not the slightest doubt of what had happened.

He was firing a ray of intolerable energy.

As he crouched, he was conscious for the first time of the quiet confidence that was in him, the certainties. Unlike anything he had ever known, a sense of destiny.

He waited for the next attack from the unsuspecting enemy, and became aware of another unusualness.

It required a moment to understand what it was: silence!

Clair frowned; and then again he nodded to himself in perfect comprehension. There was no roar of engines. Which was utterly natural: the spaceship that had been NA-7044 wouldn't be using gasoline engines.

It glided on with a glasslike smoothness, a superb armoured creature of deep space, idling along with an impregnable casualness.

Clair stood up, and slipped into the seat before the duplicate controls. 'I'll take over,' he said very gently to Wilson. 'You get to the medicine kit, and do something for that arm. We'll land in a few minutes.'

As he finished speaking, his eyes searched the controls; and he smiled with a sudden, heart-quickening glee. The controls, though they were almost the same, were a shade different. The difference between life and death.

The accelerator was like some supersensitive pressure gauge; it reacted to the barest touch. With boldness Clair pressed it hard – and reeled from a moment of ultra-speed. He saw the great, familiar sweep of England's shore.

They came down with scarcely a jar. The crescent moon was a pale shadow in the middle-western sky, as Clair stepped to the ground beside Colonel Ingraham.

146

The colonel swelled a little. 'We certainly made it hot for those Boches. I blew two of them up myself. Must have set off their bomb nests.'

For an instant, the officer's utter obliviousness to what had really happened, was startling. But actually, Clair thought finally, it explained something that had been puzzling:

The superman had been able to materialize because Professor Capper *had* identified his origin, but, more than that, because the scientist had, in his superb death, provided an intense source of nervous exaltation – the purest of energies.

Enough energy around which to project, not only a dynamic will, but a concrete spaceship.

Why was the spaceship still here? That had been the puzzling thing until Colonel Ingraham spoke, and which now was as clear as light:

The people of freedom's great future, the only world now, were not simply trusting to the fact that a flight, which had once failed, had, by their intervention, succeeded.

Men were too obstinate, too blind, too practical; so –

The superman that had been Squadron Leader Ernest William Clair smiled a secret smile. He was here to see that a world would be born – properly.

THE STAR-SAINT

As he passed the two women in the corridor of the spaceship
Colonist 12, Leonard Hanley heard one of them say:

'He was on the far side of the galaxy, and came here when
he heard about our trouble. He doesn't need spaceships to
travel, you know . . .'

Hanley walked on, cynical and annoyed. As leader of the
colonists, he'd been advised two hours before by Captain
Cranston that Mark Rogan had arrived. The commanding
officer's memo had stated, among other things:

'Since we will reach the planet Ariel, our destination,
within half an Earth day, we are fortunate that the Space
Patrol's great alien communications expert was available to
help us. Mr Rogan's presence means that you and your
people can make your landing at once, regardless of what
may have happened to the first settlement . . . and the ship
can leave.'

The reference to the ship departing immediately made
Hanley grim. 'Oh, no, you don't, Captain,' he thought.
'You're not leaving till we find out what's happened down
there.'

He continued along the corridor to the radio room,
looked in through the window, and saw that the operator on
duty was a young man named Farde. 'Anything new?'
Hanley asked.

The operator turned lazily. His manner had just enough
insolence in it to be irritating, and just enough deference to
make it difficult to take offence.

'Same old repetition of our messages,' he said.

Hanley hesitated. Time had been when he had tried to break
down this barrier between crew and passengers. He'd felt
that, in a long, two-year voyage, there shouldn't be con-
straint or hostility. Yet, in the end, he'd given up. To the
crew members, the eight hundred colonists – men, women

and children – were 'emigrants.' They had no lower term applicable to human beings.

Hanley, who was an engineer, and who had been a university professor, had often thought the crew members were not a prepossessing lot.

Once more, he hesitated, remembering the two women who had gossiped in the corridor about the mysterious Mark Rogan. He said casually: 'We were lucky to get hold of Mark Rogan.'

'Yep.'

'When,' asked Hanley, 'did he first get in touch with you?'

'Oh, that wouldn't be through here, sir.'

'How do you mean?' Sharply. 'Don't you get all radio messages here?'

'Well – yes, in a sense.' The operator hesitated. 'Fact is, Mr Rogan doesn't answer regular calls. You broadcast your problem. He comes only if he's interested.'

'He just arrives, is that it?'

'That's correct.'

'Thanks,' said Hanley in a subdued voice.

He was quietly furious as he walked on. The set-up shrieked of the phoniness of a man who allowed people to believe that he was supernormal. So he didn't use spaceships to travel through space! And he helped only if something interested him!

Hanley's anger subsided abruptly. It struck him with a shock that Rogan's coming had sinister significance. Because he *had* come.

Hanley reached his own apartment; and Eleanora, his wife, was serving lunch to himself and the two children when a wall communicator switched on, and a voice announced:

'Attention, all passengers and crew. We are entering the atmosphere of Ariel. Captain Cranston has called a meeting in the auditorium for one hour from now to discuss landing.'

Hanley sat awkwardly in a chair on the auditorium platform, and uneasily watched the angry colonists. It seemed hard to believe right now that they had elected him their leader. For he realized they must land regardless of the danger on the planet below; and that was a reality that most of the colonists did not seem to be facing.

They were shouting furiously, shaking their first at Captain Cranston, who stood at the front of the platform. The roar of their voices filled the small room, and echoed from the halls beyond, where other people crowded, listening to the loudspeaker.

Despite his own tension, Hanley kept being distracted by the stranger who sat in the chair beside him. Rogan, he guessed. It could be no other on this ship, where everyone knew everyone else.

Even with his foreknowledge, there would have been reasons for noticing the man. Rogan was slim of build, about five feet ten inches tall; and Hanley had heard him say something to Captain Cranston in a voice so soft, so gentle, that he had felt a thickening of dislike in his throat. The stranger had eyes as green as emeralds, an unusual colour for a human being.

With a faint distaste, Hanley turned away from the man and studied the viewing plate at the rear of the platform. It was quite a large plate, and a sizeable area of the ground below was visible on it.

The picture was not clear at this height, yet it was sharp enough to show green vegetation. To the left was the silvery gleam of a winding river. To the right were the ruins of the first human settlement on the planet Ariel.

Hanley studied the scene unhappily. As a scientist and administrator, he felt no personal fear at anything that might develop below. But when he thought of Eleanora and the children, his feelings about the landing became mixed up.

The audience quieted at last. At the front of the stage, Captain Cranston said: 'I admit an unfortunate situation has arisen. I cannot explain how, on an apparently uninhabited planet, a human colony has been destroyed. But I must land you. We haven't enough food to take back such a large group. I regret it, but here you are and here you must remain. But now – ' he half turned – 'I want to introduce you to a man who came aboard ship today. Mark Rogan, one of the great men of the Space Patrol, is here to help you. Mr Rogan, will you come over here to be introduced. And you, also, Mr Hanley.'

As Rogan came up, the officer said, 'Mr Rogan, please say a few words to these unhappy people.'

Rogan looked at them for a moment, then smiled, and

150

said in the same gentle voice Hanley had already heard:

'Folks, everything will be all right. Have no fear. I've listened to these radio repetitions, and I feel confident that in a day or so I'll be able to give you the signal that means safe landings.'

He stepped back. There was dead silence; and then all over the auditorium women sighed. Hanley, who had listened in amazement to the sugary reassurance, stared at the audience, baffled. Anxious, too. He had heard Mark Rogan had an unsavoury reputation where women were concerned.

Captain Cranston was speaking again, conversationally: 'Len, I want you to meet Mark Rogan.' To Rogan, he said: 'Mr Hanley is leader of the colonists.'

The vividly green eyes seemed to study Hanley's face. Rogan smiled finally, and held out a slender hand. Hanley grasped it grudgingly, and instinctively squeezed hard on the long, tapering fingers.

Rogan's smile sharpened slightly, and he returned the pressure. Hanley felt as though his hand had been caught in a vice. He turned pale with the pain of it. In agony, he let go. Instantly, the other's grip relaxed also. Momentarily, thoughtfully now, the green eyes examined him again. Hanley had the unhappy conviction that his enmity had been evaluated, and that he had lost the first round.

Captain Cranston was facing the audience. 'Ladies and gentlemen, the exploratory landings will be made by armed craft under the joint command of Mr Rogan and Mr Hanley. There's still time for a descent today, so let's make our preparations.'

* * * * *

Into the crewboat Hanley loaded a walkie-talkie, a Geiger-counter, a ground radar instrument, and a gadget that could make vibrations all the way from sound waves through the ultra-sonic range on up to short wave radio.

From the corner of one eye, he saw Rogan coming along the corridor. He turned away hastily, then – as quickly – looked again. And his first impression was right. The man wore slacks and a shirt that was open at the neck. His pockets did not bulge with gadgets. His hands were empty. He carried no visible equipment.

Rogan nodded a greeting which Hanley curtly acknowl-
edged. As Rogan stepped into the crewboat, Hanley thought
satirically:

'At least he's condescending to travel by ordinary
transportation.'

It was about ten minutes later that the small craft came to
rest in the middle of the desolation that had been a settlement of one thousand people.

As Hanley climbed shakily to the ground, one of the crew
members said: 'The place looks as if it'd been worked over
by a bulldozer.'

Hanley had to swallow as he stared at the shambles.
Somebody, or something, had gone to a lot of trouble. The
buildings, which had been made of field stone, were so
thoroughly demolished that even the individual stones had
been scattered. Here and there, grass was beginning to grow
again. Except for that, and except for a few large trees, as far
as he could see, the land had been ploughed raw as if by a
gigantic scraper.

Hanley strode forward, stumbled over something, looked
down, and drew back hastily. He had stepped on what was
left of a human being. The flesh and bone had been ground
into the soil.

He saw now that there were bodies all over among the
wreckage. It was not always easy to make them out. Many
of them seemed a part of the ground, so completely had they
been smashed, and pushed in, and covered with dirt.

Frank Stratton, a young colonist, came over and stood
beside him. Hanley turned and called to Rogan:

'I think we should take a quick look over this territory,
Mr Rogan. How about you and me walking down by the
river, while Mr Stratton and – ' he named a colonist
technician – 'go into those hills. The others can pair up to
suit themselves. No directives to anyone. Just report what
you see, and turn back in two hours or less.'

Hanley didn't wait for agreement, but hurried over to the
crewboat. It would be unusual for the two leaders of a group
to go off together, but he was determined to see an alien
communications expert at work. In the back of his mind he
had already decided to try to solve the problem himself,
without help from the 'expert'.

He lifted his pack of instruments out of the boat, and slung it over his shoulder. The weight of the load made him stagger, but he leaned into it; and presently Rogan and he were walking away from the shattered remnants of the settlement. Hanley was surprised that the other had yielded so readily to his suggestion. He noticed that Rogan kept looking into the sky, and only once or twice paused to study the ground.

The hard, gravelly soil gave way to smooth, lawn-like grass. The stones and boulders that had been everywhere around the destroyed village, disappeared. They came to the first considerable grove of trees. Some bore fruit. Others were blossom-filled. A sweet fragrance permeated the clear, warm air.

They reached the river, a wide stream that flowed with an oily slickness suggesting depth and speed. They followed a natural pathway along the foot of an ever steeper shore till finally the bank was a hundred foot high overhanging cliff. From ahead, now, came the roaring sound of water tumbling over falls.

Rogan, who was slightly ahead, paused; and Hanley chose the opportunity to lower his heavy pack and set up his instruments. The Geiger-counter had not clicked once, so he laid it on the ground out of the way. He spoke briefly into the walkie-talkie, and it roared back at him a babble of signals.

It was not a pleasant feeling, listening to that confusion of calls. Aboard ship, the effect had been eerie. Here several miles from the village, it gave Hanley a queasy sensation.

He was suddenly dissatisfied with their position. 'Mr Rogan,' he called, 'don't you think we're in a rather vulnerable spot?'

Rogan did not turn, nor did he show in any way that he had heard the question. Hanley flushed and, abruptly furious, walked over to him. 'We'll have this out right now!' he thought.

As he came up, he saw that the other was staring down at a small area of sand. It reminded Hanley that Rogan had paused twice previously, and both times had looked at similar patches of sand.

The discovery briefly drained Hanley's anger. He had been

looking for a pattern in Rogan's activity; and here it was. He stopped, and studied the area. It looked like ordinary sand, a greyish yellow-brown in colour, quite unassuming, and about as unlikely a source of life as anything he had ever seen.

Hanley hesitated. He wanted to ask questions, but the man was so discourteous that he hesitated to expose himself to further insults. He half-turned away – and then saw that Rogan was looking at him. Rogan said in his soft voice:

'Mr Hanley, I sense in your attitude that you spoke to me a short time ago, and that you are incensed because I did not answer. Is that correct?'

Hanley nodded, not trusting himself to speak. The wording seemed to imply – he couldn't decide, but it restimulated his anger. 'Sense in your attitude,' indeed. Was Rogan trying to suggest that he had *not* heard the words? Hanley waited, fuming.

Rogan went on, 'I find myself in this situation so often that, for the most part, I do not bother to explain it any more.' His green eyes glowed as with a light of their own. 'However, since it may be necessary for us to co-operate in the coming crisis, I ask you to believe me when I say that I do not hear when I am concentrating. I shut off all extraneous phenomena.' He finished gently, 'If that statement violates your sense of reality, I'm sorry.'

Hanley said grudgingly, 'I've heard of such things. Hypnosis.'

'If you need a label,' said Rogan, and his tone was almost indifferent, 'that's as good as any. But, actually, it is not the answer.'

Belatedly, it struck Hanley that the other had made an effort to be friendly. He said quickly, 'Thank you, Mr Rogan, I appreciate the explanation. But would you mind telling me, what are you looking for in that sand?'

'Life.' Rogan was turning away. 'Life in so simple a state that it is generally not even thought of as such. You see, Mr Hanley, every planet has its own initial life-process, the state where inorganic matter and organic are almost indistinguishable. This process goes on continuously; and it is the building block of all subsequent life on that particular world. I cannot prove this to you. There is no instrument I know of except my own brain for detecting its existence. You will not immediately realize to what extent that fact rules my actions. And so, I suggest that you do *not* start feeling friendly toward me because I have made this rather involved explanation. You'll probably regret it.'

Hanley, who was already disposed to be more friendly, felt uneasy. It seemed clear that Rogan meant exactly what he had said.

He saw that the man was looking at the sand. Hanley turned, and strode back to his instruments. He thought: 'After all, I ought to be able to locate the larger life forms without knowing anything about the building blocks – and in that department mechanical equipment may be very useful.'

He set up his ground radar device, and began to send signals straight down. He aimed the signals in various directions and, once, obtained a reaction which indicated the existence of a tiny cave – it was a mere pocket, and unimportant.

He repacked the radar instrument, and began to tune the vibration machine. The response needle leaped suddenly. There was a shout from Rogan: 'Hanley – jump – this way!'

Hanley heard a crashing sound above him, and involuntarily looked up. He yelled hoarsely as he saw the rock, only feet away. He tried to duck – and there was a stunning blow, an instant of unbearable pain, and blackness.

Pain. His head ached and ached. With a groan, Hanley opened his eyes. He was lying beneath the overhanging edge of the rocky cliff, a few feet from where he had been when the rock struck him.

The sound of the nearby waterfall was loud in his ears. Instinctively, before he remembered that it was still out of sight, he strained to locate it. He succeeded only in getting a better view of the visible part of the ledge, where Rogan had been before the rock struck him.

Rogan was not in sight.

Hanley climbed to his feet. His equipment was lying to his left, the radar device on its side, smashed. Ignoring it, he walked along the ledge past it to where there was a sharp turn. That gave him a view of nearly a mile of the river's curving bank. There was not a movement anywhere that he could see.

155

Puzzled, and beginning to be angry, Hanley walked in the other direction nearly two hundred yards. He saw the falls suddenly around a bend. The water dropped more than a hundred feet to the beginning of a great valley. A forest came down to the river's edge, and stretched away into the distance, a green and brown vista.

Nowhere was there a sign of Rogan.

Hanley returned to get his things, undecided as to what his next move should be. He felt impelled to go on. And yet, unquestionably, the rock had missed killing him by milli-metres. There was caked blood on the side of his head, and his cheek burned where the skin had been scraped off.

He was momentarily relieved to discover a note stuck in the handle of the Geiger-counter. 'The guy's human after all,' he thought.

Then he read the note. It said: 'Go back to the ship! I'll be gone for a day or two.'

Hanley compressed his lips, and the flush that mounted to his cheeks was not all fever from his wound. Yet, once more, his anger died away. Rogan was not responsible for him; and his job on this planet did not require that he look after injured people.

Hanley switched on the walkie-talkie. The earphones were alive with sounds. His own voice, in jumbled messages that he'd sent from the ship more than a week before, was part of the crescendo of noise. Half a dozen times, he tried to send an SOS, giving his position. The appeal was taken up, and lost among the rest.

There was nothing to do but start along the trail back . . . He reached the village just before dark, and was immediately taken up to the ship. Both doctors insisted that he spend the night in the hospital ward, though they reported reassuringly that he would probably be all right in the morning.

Hanley slept fitfully. Once, he waked up and thought: 'At least he's a courageous man. He's down there alone, at night.'

It justified to some extent his own lie to the others. He had told them that Rogan had gone on only after assuring himself that Hanley was not seriously hurt. Rogan had done nothing of the kind. But it was essential that the colonists continue to trust him.

Some time during the night Hanley's strength and energy

156

came back. About dawn, he opened his eyes in tense excitement. That rock! Its fall had been no accident. Somebody or something had shoved it down upon him.

'I'll go out there in the morning,' he decided.

He was dressing when his wife came in, about nine o'clock. She walked over to a chair, and sank into it. Her fine grey eyes looked tired. Her long blonde hair had not been properly arranged. There were lines in her face.

'I've been worried,' she said drably.

'I'm all right,' Hanley spoke reassuringly. 'I was only bruised a little and shaken.'

She seemed not to hear. 'When I think of him down there with the fate of the whole colony depending on his remaining alive – '

Briefly, it shocked Hanley to realize that her anxiety was for Rogan, not himself. She looked up unhappily.

'Len, do you think it was wise of you to let him go on alone?'

Hanley stared at her in amazement, but made no reply. It seemed to him that there was no adequate comment to make to that. Nevertheless, as he ate breakfast, he felt more determined than ever to solve this problem before Rogan.

A few minutes later, with Frank Stratton at the controls of the crewboat, he set out once more for the river. His plan of action was simplicity itself: If there was life here, it would show itself in some way. An observant man should be able to find it without having a special type of brain.

* * * * *

They came down in a meadow half a mile from the river and about a mile from the waterfall. It seemed a sufficiently central position from which to examine the rock-throwing episode.

Young Stratton, who had been silent during the flight said suddenly, 'Pretty country – if it weren't for the stones.'

Hanley nodded absently. He climbed down to the ground, and then paused for another survey of the countryside. Trees, miles of green grass, gaily coloured flowers, the silvery gleam of the waterfall, and the great forested valley beyond it – here was natural beauty in abundance.

True, as Stratton had pointed out, there were small rocks

157

in plenty, but they could be removed. Hanley walked to the nearest one, and picked it up. It was about the size of a large melon, and unexpectedly light in weight. He stood holding it, watching the sunlight flash over its surface.

At first glance, it seemed to be granite, the bright reflecting surfaces suggesting mica specks. On closer examination, Hanley wasn't so sure. He saw that his fingers were already stained yellow. Sulphur, he guessed. And in rather free form.

Behind him, Stratton said sullenly, 'This fellow, Rogan – who is he! I mean, is there some special reason why the women have to go silly over him? Dorothy kept me awake half the night worrying about his being down here alone.'

Intent though he had been on the stone, Hanley recalled the similar reaction of Eleanora, and half turned. 'He's the only one of his kind,' he began, 'except for – ' He stopped. For the rest was rumour only. He went on slowly, 'According to reports, his parents were wrecked on some uninhabited planet, and he was born there while they were repairing the ship. He was still a child when they took him away, and by the time they began to suspect he was different, it was too late.'

'Too late for what?'

'They had no idea where the planet was on which they'd been wrecked.'

'Oh!' The blond youth was silent. Hanley was about to return his attention to the stone when Stratton said, 'What's this story about his having children all over the galaxy?'

'Another rumour.'

Hanley spoke curtly. It gave him no pleasure to defend Mark Rogan, especially when his own mind was uneasy with the same suspicions as Stratton was experiencing.

'What's he trying to do?' asked the young man grimly. 'Produce a bunch of freaks like himself?'

That was so exactly the way he had originally heard it that Hanley swallowed. In spite of himself, he said sarcastically, 'Maybe he believes his wild talent for dealing with non-human races should be spread as widely as possible. Particularly, I imagine, he feels that when his services have been called for, the women of the new colony should be only too willing to provide perceptive children and so secure the future of the human race on that planet. It – '

He came to an abrupt stop, startled. He had intended to

be ironic, but abruptly the notion sounded plausible. *And necessary.*

'My God!' he thought, 'it he ever comes near Eleanora, I'll – '

In abrupt tension, he raised the rock in his hands above his head, and flung it down upon another one nearby. There was a loud, cracking sound. Both stones shattered, and a chance wind blew a cloud of yellowish dust into his face. The smell of sulphur was momentarily unbearably strong. Hanley coughed, almost choked, and then he had backed out into fresher air.

He was about to bend down over the broken pieces of the two stones, when Stratton let out a yell. 'Mr Hanley – the rocks – they're moving!'

In that first moment of mental confusion, Hanley had several fantastic impressions. Unquestionably, stones all over the meadow were beginning to roll towards them, slowly, as if they were not exactly sure of their direction – but they *were* rolling. Simultaneously, the wind that had been merely a series of gusts until then, began to blow at gale proportions. Dead leaves whirled into his face. Small pieces of grit stung his cheeks.

Hanley's eyes began to water. Through a blur, he made his way to the crewboat, and fumbled for the steps that led to the deck. The wind was so strong now that he had to bend into it to remain on his feet. From above him, young Stratton yelled: 'This way – quick!'

A hand caught Hanley's shoulder, guiding him. A moment later he was scrambling up the steps, and had flung himself prostrate beside his companion. He lay there for a minute, gasping. Then he saw Stratton wriggling towards the controls.

Hanley shouted at him, 'Frank – wait!'

The blond youth turned, and said earnestly: 'Mr Hanley, we'd better get out of here. We might be blown over on our side.'

His words were tossed by the wind, distorted, and delivered finally half-faded, but still comprehensible. Hanley shook his head stubbornly.

'Can't you see?' he shouted. 'These stones are the life-form! We've got to stay and find out things about them. If we can get enough information we won't need Rogan.'

It stopped the young man. He turned a contorted face towards Hanley. 'By Heaven,' he said, 'we'll show that – '

His whole body twisted with eagerness. Hanley called to him. 'Turn on the radio! Let's see what's coming over.'

The radio was alive with voices. Wherever Stratton turned the dial, he produced uproar that was loud and continuous. Hanley listened grimly for a minute, and then glanced over the side of the boat.

He winced as he saw that the stones were piling up against the side of the small vessel, one on top of the other. The pile, at its highest point, was about three feet from the ground. It sloped back to a thin line of pebbles some twelve to fifteen feet from the bigger stones at the front. Hanley estimated that there were several hundred stones already in the pile.

More were coming. He flinched, but kept on looking. As far as he could see over that wind-swept meadow, stones were rolling towards the crewboat. Their speed seemed to vary according to their size. He judged that the medium-sized ones were travelling two or three miles per hour, whereas several that were almost two feet in diameter were moving at nearer five miles per hour.

The pile grew even as he watched. Hanley turned uneasily toward Stratton. And saw that the young man was pushing with a stick at something that seemed to be threatening him from the other side of the small craft.

Stratton turned, 'The stones!' he yelled hoarsely. 'They've piled up. They'll be spilling on top of us in a minute.'

Hanley hesitated. It seemed to him that by remaining they had learned how the enemy attacked. Perhaps, if they stayed just a bit longer –

His thought was interrupted by another shout from young Stratton: 'Mr Hanley – look!'

Hanley followed the young man's pointing hand. A giant rock was lifting itself out of the ground a hundred feet away. It was at least ten feet in diameter, and it was poising now, turning, as if trying by means of some alien senses to decide its direction. In a moment it would be bearing down on them.

Hanley gulped, and then in a loud yet calm voice said, 'All right – lift her up!'

As Stratton manipulated the drive control lever, there was a surge of power that sent a vibratory impulse through the rigid metals of the ship. The deck throbbed under Hanley, and he could almost feel the engines straining to lift the craft.

'*Mr Hanley, something is holding us down!*'

Hanley thought blankly: 'We'll have to get out and run. But where to?'

He was about to say, 'Try again!' when he saw that the huge rock was starting to move. Straight at the ship it came, gathering speed each time it turned over.

Hanley shouted, 'Frank – the big rock – come this way!'

He didn't wait to see if the young man obeyed. With a convulsive effort, he flung himself far out over the side of the craft. He landed on the rock he had aimed at, and, using it as a spring board, leaped again.

Behind him, there was a crash, a squealing of metal and the shriek of a human being in mortal agony.

And silence.

* * * * *

He was running, with a dying wind lending wings to his feet. Hanley finally slowed from exhaustion, and looked back. He had gone about two hundred and fifty yards; and there were several trees and much shrubbery between him and the crewboat. But he could see that the rock was still lying on top of the smashed craft. He noticed no movement anywhere. Even the stones were still.

The great wind blew in gusts only now. It was spent. Already, the incident had a dream-like quality. It seemed incredible that Frank Stratton was lying dead or desperately injured in the wreck of the boat. Hanley thought distractedly: 'I've got to go back.'

A hundred feet from him, a small stone stirred, lifted itself out of its hole, and started hesitantly toward him. Simultaneously, there was other movement. Scores of stones began to move in his direction.

Hanley retreated. He had an empty feeling about what had happened to his companion. But far more important was the fact that he had found the hostile life-form on this planet. He had to get back to the ship with that vital information.

He headed on a course parallel to the river toward the

village, which he judged was three or four miles away. In a few minutes he had outdistanced the moving stones. 'They're slow,' he thought exultantly. 'It takes a little while for them to decide that somebody is around.'

He began to picture the life of the colonists on this frontier planet. They'd have to clear rocks from whole areas. Atoguns with their thousand-unit explosive charges to a loading would be standard equipment for men and women alike. It was even possible to visualize a time when the curious rock-life would be of museum interest only. They must have a very slow growth, and so could probably be eliminated from all except the most remote territories within a measurable time.

He was still considering the possibilities when he saw a solid glitter of stones ahead.

Hanley stopped, chilled. Hastily, he turned from the river. And stopped again. The stony glitter was in that direction also.

Swallowing, he headed for the river. His eyes searched for stones in that direction. A few moving objects were visible among the shrubbery, but there was so much brush and scrubwood that it seemed evident that small rocks would have difficulty in making progress. That became his hope, instantly.

He hurried past several large trees, sizing them up for girth as he went by. The largest tree in the vicinity he found less than two hundred feet from the cliff's edge.

One section of its huge trunk sloped up from the ground at so gradual a slant that he'd be able to run up it swiftly, scramble up to another thick branch, and from there go almost to the top of the main trunk which towered majestically above any other tree in the neighbourhood.

Hanley hurried to the edge of the cliff overlooking the river. The water was nearly fifty feet below, and the wall of the cliff ran sheerly down. It even slanted inward slightly; and there was no possibility of climbing down with a ladder. One look convinced Hanley that the river did not offer a way of escape.

As he headed back toward the tree, he saw uneasily that more than a score of stones had rolled between him and the

162

safety of the trunk. He walked straight toward one of them. It kept rolling in the same direction after he had stepped over it, and did not stop until he had gone past two more of the blind things. Then it halted, and began hesitantly to move toward him again.

His fear faded even more. He took a quick look around to make sure that he was not being hemmed in. Then he waited for the stone to come up to him. As it approached, he studied it anxiously for a sign of intelligence. There was nothing but the smoothly porous, rock-like substance.

It rolled right up against his foot, touched his boot – and attached itself.

He kicked at it, but it clung as if it were glued to the boot. It weighed at least five pounds, and when he moved his foot he felt the drag of it, the need to strain his muscles in order to lift it, the sharp fear that he wouldn't be able to get rid of it.

Other stones were approaching. Alarmed, Hanley retreated to the tree trunk, and, bending down, removed the boot to which the rock had attached itself. He shook the boot, vainly. With abrupt determination, he raised it above his head, and flung it, boot and stone together, straight down on another stone.

The two rocks dissolved; there was a gust of wind that blew the sulphurous dust into his face. Hanley coughed furiously. When he could see again through his tear-filled eyes, he was first attracted to a gleaming crystal that lay in the pile of debris. He studied it, then hastily he recovered his boot, and started up the trunk.

It was time. As far as the eye could see, the land glittered with the movement of stones converging towards him.

His day in the tree passed eneventfully.

Just before dark, Hanley climbed to a higher branch and found himself a reasonably comfortable crotch for the night. He spent the early hours of darkness wide awake, alert to sounds below. About midnight, he dozed.

He awakened with a start. The sun was just coming up over the horizon – and a crewboat was speeding toward him, following the course of the river. He jumped hastily to his feet, almost fell out of the tree as a thick branch broke like so much dead wood. And then, safely balanced again, he tore off his coat and shirt.

He began to wave the shirt frantically . . .

As Eleanora served him breakfast Hanley learned that
Mark Rogan had returned to the ship the evening before,
spent the night aboard, and departed at dawn. He stopped
eating, and considered the news. Finally:

'Did he have anything to say? Had he solved the problem?'

He waited, jealous of his own discovery, anxious not to
have been out-done. Eleanora sighed; then:

'I don't think so. Of course, he talked mostly to the men.
Perhaps he gave them private information.'

Hanley doubted it. And so, by the simple process of going
out and looking, an ordinary man had bested the famous
communications expert.

He was about to resume eating when the odd tone in
which his wife had spoken made him look up. 'He talked
mostly to the men?' he echoed.

There was a flush on her face. She said, 'I had him to
dinner.' She added quickly, 'I expected you back. It didn't
occur to me that you – '

She sounded so defensive that he felt compelled to
interrupt: 'It's all right, my dear. I understand, I understand.'

He wasn't sure that he did. As he continued to eat, he
studied her unobtrusively, shaken by his thoughts. Once he
almost said: 'Are you sure that he didn't also spend the
night?' The insult of the thought was so outrageous that he
cringed, and felt angry at himself.

But it decided him. He had been intending to wait, and
learn what Rogan had discovered; the problem of dealing
with the rock-life was by no means solved. But he found
himself suddenly less amenable to that kind of reasoning.

He discovered that the other leaders, once they heard the
detailed account of his experience, were equally reluctant to
wait.

'Our women have gone crazy about that man,' one
individual said angrily. 'Do you know what my wife
suggested when she heard that Frank Stratton was dead?
She thought his widow ought to marry Rogan right away,
before he went away. Of course, from all accounts, he's not

164

the marrying kind. But just imagine having such an idea instantly.'

'It's a survival instinct,' said another man. 'History is full of stories of women who have wanted their children to be fathered by famous men. In this case, with Rogan's special ability – '

'Not so special,' somebody interrupted. 'Our own leader, Leonard Hanley, discovered the enemy without any help from the famous man.'

Hanley ended the somewhat heated discussion finally by saying, 'It will take us most of today to get our main equipment down. If Mr Rogan condescends to turn up before we're ready to disembark the women and children, he can offer his views at that time. Otherwise – '

Mark Rogan, as it happened, did not condescend to turn up.

The landings were made in open areas along the river bank in the forested valley below the falls. By noon, everybody was on the ground. Hanley had a final consultation with Captain Cranston, and was informed that the Colonist twelve would leave immediately.

'We've already been far too long on this trip,' the officer said in justification. 'The owners will be furious.'

Hanley could feel no sympathy for the gentlemen, but he recognized that he and the others would experience the grimmer effects of that commercialism. He tried to think of something that would delay the ship's departure, but all that occurred to him finally was:

'What about Mr Rogan? Aren't you going to wait for him?'

Captain Cranston shrugged. 'A patrol ship will probably pick him up. Well, goodbye.'

As they shook hands, Hanley thought cynically that there was no suggestion now that Rogan could travel through space without spaceships. It seemed amazing that anyone could have believed such nonsense.

Midafternoon. Out of the corner of one eye, Hanley saw Eleanora – who had been working beside the tent – snatch a compact from a pocket of her slacks, and hastily start to powder her face. Hanley glanced in the direction she had

165

been gazing, and winced. Mark Rogan was coming toward him along the river bank.

The Patrol man said nothing until he was less than half a dozen feet from Hanley. Then: 'Where's the ship? Mr Hanley, did you order this landing?'

His voice was as soft as it had always been, but there was an edge of suppressed anger in it that chilled Hanley despite his confidence. The thought came: 'Have I possibly made a mistake?'

Aloud, he said, 'Yes, I ordered the landing. It just happens, Mr Rogan – ' he was beginning to feel sure of himself again – 'that I discovered the nature of the hostile life on this planet, and we have taken all necessary precautions.'

Twice, Rogan seemed about to speak, but finally he stepped back. There was an enigmatic smile on his face as he looked around at the busy colonists. Several trees and been chopped down, and they were now in the process of being converted to plastic.

Silently, Rogan walked over to the complex machinery, and watched the bubbling up of the sap in the wood as it was sawed, and then the swift chemical action that neutralized the resinous substance.

He came back to Hanley, and his vividly green eyes seemed to glow with irony, as he said, 'What *did* you discover?'

He listened with his head slightly tilted to one side, as if he were hearing more than the words. And his eyes had a faraway look in them; he seemed to be gazing at a scene that was in his mind. He said finally, 'You think then that the crystal you saw in the rock after you had smashed it was possibly the "brain"?'

Hanley hesitated; then defensively, 'The piezo-electric crystal is the heart of radio and television engineering, and in a certain sense crystals grow, and – '

He got no further. Eleanora had run forward and grasped Rogan by the arm. 'Please,' she begged, 'what's wrong? What's the matter?'

Rogan released himself gently from her fingers. 'Mrs Hanley,' he said quietly, 'your husband has made a deadly dangerous error. The stone activity is merely a product of the scientific control which the ruling intelligence of this planet exercises over its environment.'

He turned to the stricken Hanley. 'Was there a strong wind at any time while you were being attacked?'

Hanley nodded mutely.

Rogan said, 'Another manifestation.'

He looked at his watch, and said, 'It's a little more than two hours till dark. If we take only essentials, we can be out of this valley before the sun sets.'

He paused. His green eyes fixed on Hanley's wavering gaze with a bleak intensity. He said curtly, 'Give the command!'

'B – but – ' Hanley stammered his reaction, then pulled himself together. 'It's impossible. Besides, we've got to make our stand somewhere. We – '

He stopped hopelessly, already convinced, but too miserable to go on.

Rogan said, 'Give the order, and I'll explain – '

Shortly after night fell, a gale wind sprang up. It blew for an hour, sand filled, stinging their faces as they walked behind the long rows of caterpillar tractors. All the younger children were taken up in the six crewboats. When the storm was past, several of the healthier children were brought down, and their places in the boats taken by women who could no longer remain awake.

About midnight, the attack of the stones began. Rocks twenty and thirty feet in diameter thundered out of the darkness into the range of the groping searchlight beams, which were mounted on the tractors. Before the extent of the assault could be gauged, two of the tractors were crushed. Metal screeched, men shrieked in dismayed agony – and mounted atoguns pulverized the rocks before any more damage could be done.

Several people had to be rescued from small stones that attached themselves to shoes and boots, and prevented all except the most awkward movement. When that was over, Hanley had to walk among the weary men and women, and insist that Rogan's directive to 'keep moving' be obeyed.

Just before dawn, the ground under them began to heave and shake. Great fissures opened, and individuals had terrifying experiences before they were pulled to safety out of suddenly created abysses.

As the faint light of day broke through the blackness of the horizon, Hanley mumbled to Rogan, 'You mean – they can cause sustained earthquakes of *that* proportion?'

Rogan said, 'I don't think that will happen very often. I think it requires great courage for them to penetrate hot rock areas where such phenomena can be stirred up.'

He broke off, thoughtfully: 'I see this as an ally arrangement, with the onus being on man to prove that he can be helpful. Of course, it will take a while – after this unfortunate beginning – to persuade the Intelligence to consider such an arrangement. It doesn't think in human terms.'

Hanley was intent. 'Let me get this clear. You're taking us to a flat plain north of here. You want us to build concrete huts there while we wait for you to persuade the Intelligence that we mean no harm. Is that right?'

Rogan said, 'It'd be better if you kept moving. But of course that would be very difficult . . . with women . . . children.' He seemed to be arguing with himself.

Hanley persisted, 'But we'll be reasonably safe on such a barren plain?'

'Safe!' Rogan stared at him. 'Man, you don't seem to understand. Despite the similarity to Earth appearance, this planet has a different life process. You're going to learn what that means.'

Hanley felt too humble to ask any more questions. An hour later, he watched as Rogan commandeered one of the crewboats, and flew off into the morning mists. About noon, Hanley dispatched the other crewboats to rescue some of the equipment they had abandoned the night before.

The boats came back about dark with a weird report. A barrel of salt meat had rolled away from them, and had evaded all their efforts to capture it. An atomic jet proved a hazard. It would start up, and lift itself into the air, and then shut off and fall back to the ground, only to repeat the process. It almost wrecked a crewboat before a magnetic crane mounted on another boat lifted it permanently clear of the ground. Thereafter it remained lifeless.

Hanley guessed unhappily: 'Tentative experiments.'

The colony spent the night on a level grassy plain. Guards patrolled the perimeter of the encampment. Tractor motors hummed and pulsed. Searchlights peered into the darkness, and all the grown-ups took turns at performing some necessary duty.

Hanley was awakened shortly after midnight by Eleanora. 'Len – my shoes.'

He examined them sleepily. The surface was all bumpy, with tiny knobs protruding through the polish. Hanley felt a grisly thrill as he realized that they were growing. He asked, 'Where did you keep them?'

'Beside me.'

'On the ground?'

'Yes.'

'You should have kept them on,' said Hanley, 'the way I did mine.'

'Leonard Hanley, I wouldn't wear shoes while I'm sleeping if it's the last – ' She stopped, said in a subdued tone, 'I'll put them on, see if they still fit.'

Later, at breakfast, he saw her limping around, tears in her eyes, but without complaint.

That afternoon one of the tractors exploded without warning, killing its driver. A flying segment tore off the arm of a five-year-old boy nearby. The women cried. The doctors eased the youngster's pain with drugs, and kept him alive. There were angry mutterings among the men. One man came over to Hanley.

'We're not going to stand for this much longer,' he said, 'We've got a right to fight back.'

Rogan turned up just before dark, and listened in silence to the account of what had happened. He said finally, 'There'll be more.'

Hanley said grimly, 'I can't understand why we don't set fire to every forest in this part of the planet, and clear the damned things from this whole area.'

Rogan, who had been turning away, faced slowly about. His eyes were almost yellow in the fading light. He said, 'Damn you, Hanley, you talk like so many scamps I've run into in my business. I tell you, you can't defeat this tree intelligence with fire, even though fire is the one thing it's afraid of. Its fear and its partial vulnerability is man's opportunity, not to destroy, but to help.'

Hanley said helplessly, 'But how does it operate? How does it control stones, and make winds and – '

'Those phenomena,' said Rogan, 'derive from the fact that its life-energy flows many times faster than ours. A nerve impulse in you and me moves approximately 300 feet a second. On this planet, it's just under 400,000. And so, even rocks have a primitive life-possibility. Crystals form easily, and can be stimulated to imitate any vibrations that affect them. Far more important, there is a constant flow of life-energy through the ground itself. The result is that everything can be affected and controlled to some extent. Divert the energy to the ground surface through grass roots and sand; and great winds rush in to cool off the "hot" surfaces. Divert it through one of our tractors and – '

'But,' said Hanley, who had been frowning, 'why didn't that tree I was on for a whole day and night – why didn't it try to kill me?'

'And call attention to itself!' said Rogan with that tight smile of his. 'It might have tried something against you that would appear accidental – like the breaking of a branch that could make you fall – but nothing overt.'

He broke off, firmly, 'Mr Hanley, there is no method but co-operation. Here is what you'll probably have to be prepared to do.'

He outlined the steps, coolly, succinctly. No encroachment for several years on an area where there were trees. Definitely no use of lumber for any purpose, except such dying wood as Rogan might, by arrangement with the forest, assign to be cut. Establishment of fire-fighting equipment to help all forests in the vicinity of the colony against spontaneous fires, the pattern later to be extended over the entire planet.

When Rogan had finished, Hanley considered the plan, and found one flaw in it. He protested, 'What I'd like to know is, how are we going to maintain contact with this Intelligence after you're gone?'

As he finished speaking, he saw that Eleanora had come up beside him. In the fading light, it seemed to Hanley that she was bending forward, as if straining for Rogan's answer.

Rogan shrugged. 'Time alone,' he said, 'can resolve that problem.'

They built the village of New Earth beside a brook. There

170

were no trees anywhere in sight. According to Rogan, the small shrubs that lined the banks of the stream were but distantly related to the greater tree-life, and could be used for any purpose.

There were no less than eighteen rock attacks during the next eleven days. In one of them, a stone one hundred and ninety feet in diameter roared across the plain toward them. It smashed two houses, plunged on for a mile across the plain, and then turned back. Crewboats with atoguns successfully exploded it before it was able to return to the village.

And then one night nothing at all happened. At dawn, Mark Rogan turned up, pale and weary looking, but smiling. 'It's all right,' he said. 'You get your chance.'

Men cheered hoarsely. Women wept and tried to touch his hand. Hanley stood back, and thought: 'It's too soon to tell.'

But the days passed, and there were no more manifestations. The guards began to sleep at their posts, and finally were no longer posted. At dusk on the eighth straight day of peace, there was a knock on the door of Hanley's house. Eleanora answered, and Hanley heard her talking to someone in a low tone. The softness of the other voice made him abruptly suspicious, and he was about to get up from his chair, when the door shut, and Eleanora came back in. She was breathless.

'He's leaving!' she said.

Hanley didn't ask who. He hurried outside, and saw that Rogan was already at the outskirts of the village, a vague figure in the gathering darkness. A week later, there was still no sign of him. Among the rank and file of the colonists, the whisper was that he had gone in his fashion to some other part of the galaxy. Hanley ridiculed the story, but when he heard it soberly stated in a gathering of technicians, he realized gloomily that the legend of Mark Rogan would survive all his denials.

Two months passed. Hanley awoke one morning to find that Eleanora had slipped into the bed beside him. 'I wish to report to my lord and master,' she said airily, 'that there's going to be an addition to the Hanley clan.'

After he had kissed her, Hanley lay silent, thinking: 'If it has green eyes and jet black hair, I'll – I'll – '

171

He couldn't imagine what he'd do. He groaned inwardly in his terrible jealousy. But already at the back of his mind was the realization that the race of man would survive on one more alien planet.